# 2022 International Cultural Exchange Conference

Location: Online | Date: August 6th, 2022

*-and-*

# 2022 Youth International Environment Protection Awareness Conference

Location: Online | Date: August 7, 2022

## EDITORS OF PROCEEDINGS:

Siqi Li, Allen Bryan Suri Zheng, Kevin Zhang

Library of Congress Control Number:        2023902666

HARDBACK:          978-1-959143-30-7
PAPERBACK:         978-1-959143-29-1
EBOOK:             978-1-959143-31-4



**Ordering Information:**

For orders and inquiries, please contact:
1-888-404-1388
www.goldtouchpress.com
book.orders@goldtouchpress.com

Printed in the United States of America

# Table of Contents

**2022 Youth International Environment Protection Awareness Conference**

# 2022 International Cultural Exchange Conference

## Introductions

Hello, and welcome to the 8th annual International Cultural Exchange Conference Focused on Teens! Our purpose is to exchange information and ideas about cultures, ranging from the United States to China, among professionals and students, as well as provide insight into education abroad. We have translated, transcribed, compiled, and edited the speeches of all our speakers.

## Acknowledgments

We would like to thank all of our guest speakers for attending and providing us with such insightful speeches. We also thank our hosts for keeping the conference running smoothly, as well as the technology department for making sure the PowerPoint was functioning properly. Thank you to all the students who translated on stage, as well as those who transcribed and translated speeches for our proceedings.

*Editors of Cultural Conference Proceedings:*
Siqi Li, Allen Bryan

*English to Chinese Translators and Interpreters:*
Siqi Li, Yiming (Amelia) Wang, Bo W.

*Proceedings Transcription:*
Siqi Li, Allen Bryan/Edward Bryan, Yiming (Amelia) Wang

*Technical Support:*
Ying Zhu

*Hosts:*
Siqi Li, Allen Bryan, Owen Ouyang, Yiming Wang, Kevin Zhang

# Eric Williams

**Eric Williams** is the founder and creative director of the Silver Room, an innovative retail, arts, education, and community events space opened in 1997. The Silver Room intersects the worlds of fashion, music, and visual art, and acts as a boutique, gallery, and community arts center. Williams is committed to creating spaces and curating events that strengthen communities and fuel positive economic impact. He holds a degree in Finance from the University of Illinois at Chicago and was a Loeb Fellow at the Graduate school of Design at Harvard University.

## African Americans' Contribution to the Arts During Uncertain Times

Transcribed by: Siqi Li

When I was at Harvard doing my fellowship, I was really thinking about how arts and culture impact communities. I was also interested in what I am doing now, a mixture of retail, arts and culture, and music, and what impact that has on our community. I was specifically thinking about the impact on the urban African American community; thinking about how our culture, music, and arts, have impacted America, and how we still impact America to this day. I want to walk you through a little bit of history, talking about Black Americans' contribution to culture and music, and how it has mirrored and impacted, in historical context, our culture's ups and downs. We tend to be a little more creative when times are turbulent. I thought that was interesting, from the days of the early 1900s to now, you see in uncertain times, how arts and culture are vibrant.

When we think about music, arts, and culture today, and how it all started, it all started in Africa, from when the first Africans came to America in the early 1600s. Two hundred years later, we see the impact that different African cultures had, during slavery, and what it looked like when slavery finally ended. Music and dancing were one of the few ways Africans could communicate with each other, especially when the plantation owners didn't understand it. We communicated through songs and dance, and sometimes silent communication. Music was a way to celebrate the little bit of time we had, usually on Sundays.

New Orleans is the city that's cited for the beginning of jazz, and Congo Square was an area where many jazz musicians would go and play. The musical influence of a people who were one generation out of slavery was astonishing: a lot of brass instruments and a lot of percussion instruments that started from Africa. This mixture of creole, French influence, and African instruments, created Jazz. A lot of this music in the very beginning was disliked by white Americans for several reasons. Number one, they felt that this music was anti-American in some ways, they saw this music was bringing people together and there was a lot of fear around what we were doing, even if we were celebrating. It was also music that brought blacks and whites together, and people that liked segregated societies didn't like the fact that music brought people together.

This music from the south, this music of enslaved people, traveled up through New Orleans, Memphis, up to New York City and Harlem, which became the epicenter of Black creativity, the epicenter of culture, the arts, literature, and music, in the 1920s-40s. This became the place for jazz, big band music, singing, and dancing, creating a stronghold in not only the US but across the world. This music was important, and all this was in New York City. Even though these bands were primarily African American bands, it was also a time when you saw the integration of Black people and white people in America who came together because of the music.

There is a very famous photo from Chicago in the 1940s showing the sophisticated way that people dressed at that time. Bronzeville is the equivalent of Harlem in NYC. The picture dates back to a lot of cultural development: new music, jazz, blues; fashion, at the time, this is the way that people dressed, so fashion has changed. Something else that's important is that this is the time when you started to see nightclubs and music venues really pop up in the big cities in America. New York was probably number one and Chicago was probably number two, and other cities across America where you would see places where people could play music. At the time, most of the clubs were segregated, which meant that Black performers couldn't go to the hotels that white people could go to, and Black performers couldn't eat in certain places where white people were allowed to eat. So even though they were performing, the idea of it being segregated was very real, they couldn't go to certain places in the south. So even though this performance and arts and culture were happening, at the same time, structural racism is still very much there.

When we speak about American music, a lot of it is Black music, be it jazz, soul, blues, or rock n' roll, I think it's important to talk about it. When we think about rock n' roll now, we think of it as traditionally white music, but it was really started by Black musicians that came out of the blues from the delta and the south, even country music. This is something that happens a lot in history, Black musicians would start something, be the founders of it, and never get credit for it or get the financial benefits from the music they started. So, to give a little historical context, rock n' roll was also historically Black music.

Now we're moving into the 60s where we talk about Motown. Motown music, another major American music, came from Detroit and it was a mixture of soul music, kind of moving away from jazz. But with Motown, it was very much music that was crafted for the appearance, making it palatable for the white American audience. From the time we started presenting albums and music, many times, we wouldn't even see a Black person on the cover of the album. They would not have Black people on the cover of an album because they feel like people wouldn't buy the music if they saw a black face. They didn't want to scare the customers. So even though sometimes you would have a Black musician, you would have a white person's face on the album/record cover. This was also the time that radios became very big, and you would hear Motown music played on the radio. Also, this music brought people together with white and Black people dancing in the nightclubs to Motown music, but some people didn't like people coming together didn't like this music.

Now we go from the 60s to the 70s, and music changed from Motown, which is really about how we can present this music to all of America and make it acceptable to people who are afraid of Black people. In the 1960s, it was all about civil rights, you had the assassination of Martin Luther King Jr., you had, in certain areas, riots and looting, and people were fearful of one another. The music was a way to make it seem less scary. The 70s became a time of Black freedom, power, and love. Even looking at how people dressed, fashion has changed: from "let's be very presentable and wear our suits" to "let's be ourselves". A lot of Black people in the 70s started to try and find links back to Africa, to their heritage, so the 70s music reflected that also, and it became a sense of freedom as a lot of the 70s music was about dancing. It was also a time when the artists started talking about the issues happening in America: civil rights, racism, and the war. Look up Marvin Gaye if you don't know who he is, but he had a lot of influential songs in the 70s, also Stevie Wonder, and James Brown. But again, it was a mixture of music for people to dance to, but also a way about consciousness, and how we can speak to the issues happening in American society, but also celebrate and dance. So, it was a very important time for music during the 70s.

So, as we move from the early 70s to the late 70s, disco music and dance music became a really big part of the culture, especially in urban areas like New York and Chicago. Music was shifting more towards celebration in many ways with the dance movement and liberation. Also, have a lot of movement in the LGBTQ+/gay culture. A lot of people that were afraid of coming out started doing that and it became more acceptable. A lot of people found that they can be themselves in nightclubs. This picture shows a really important nightclub called the Paradise Garage, where a lot of people came to dance and celebrate. Disco, coming from soul music, eventually became electronic and house music.

Immediately following the disco era, from the late 70s into the 80s, you have the birth of hip-hop in the Bronx, New York City. Hip-hop was derived from a bit of disco, a little bit of soul music, and influences from sounds back in Jamaica. People would have block parties that would happen in New York City. the music is moving from just disco and dance to a different kind of expression. How hip-hop actually started wasn't really about the MC (mic controller) or the rapper, but more about the DJ (disc jockey). In the beginning, the DJ would just play music, and they would have someone who raps with them. In the beginning, it was really just to have fun. You have the four elements of hip-hop, which are the MCing, the dancing, the graffiti, and just the culture in general. Hip-hop is really something that came out of the 70s in NYC, and you think about when something really creative comes out, it's after some seriously hard times. In the 70s in America, we went through a lot of financial problems such as high inflation and high unemployment, and New York City had a lot of crime, big blackouts, and fires everywhere, just a lot of problems. And I think that it is true that some of those problems they were having made a place more creative, and hip-hop is a creative expression that came out of this time because New York was having issues.

Now, it was important for me to talk about the history to get to today, so you know where it all came from. Artists today like Beyonce, what she's doing today is really just influenced by what happened in the past, the celebration, the nuances of arts and culture, the protests. What's happening now is a reflection of that. It's important to understand that what's happening now is not new, it happened before, and most of the artists that are doing it now are students of history. Beyonce is someone that's known worldwide, but even the sounds she's making now, like her latest album which is a house and electronic album, are basically from Chicago. Right now, when you think about Black music and American music that's now exported across the world, all of this comes from what I've talked about.

Now I want to talk about what I do and how this is all connected. I have a retail store in Chicago, and my time at Harvard was really talking about the connection between music, fashion, and design, and how they play a part together. So, what I do in my store is just a way to bring people together. We have products made by local designers, and at the very back there's a DJ booth for people to play music as they shop, and really, it's a place for discussion. It's a place for people to come in and talk about politics, arts, culture, to sports. They buy things at the store but really, it's an excuse for people to come together, like how music has brought people together.

Seventeen years ago, I started the silver Room block party. Music is very important to me, so it was important to me to have an annual celebration for all of my friends, the DJs, the MCs, and the dancers. We started having events of maybe a hundred people that exploded to forty-thousand people. Music goes back to the celebration, bringing people together, and just having a good time. Sometimes people think about black people in America with stereotypes of everybody fighting and shooting, which is not what happens. People just want to have a good time and have fun, like everywhere else in the world.

My latest business is one I've been working on for a couple of years. It is a restaurant/wine bar, in the Bronzeville neighborhood. It's a neighborhood that's been neglected in ways, not many businesses choose here and a lot of stores have closed down, but I wanted to celebrate the neighborhood so I opened up a restaurant four months ago. It's called Bronzeville Winery, a really beautiful space for the neighborhood, but is also very popular with people from all around the city coming in every day. Again, I think this is just another testament to how you can bring people together, you can do it through music, food, and wine.

The actual space has furniture made locally by an African American guy, the light fixtures are made by a friend of mine, and the artwork on the wall is made by another friend of mine, so it was important that we had local folks and friends in the community design and create this space.

This was our latest block party event I did three weeks ago, this year held on the beach in Chicago. After two years of not being able to do the event because of COVID, we came back and did an even bigger one. You could see from the smiles on people's faces that they were dancing and having a good time, once again, bringing beauty, happiness, and love to people through music and dance. I think more than ever, with COVID having everyone in the house being alone and perhaps dealing with some depression, it's important to have music to bring everyone together.

And that's it, everybody, I hope everyone gets the importance of African Americans in American music. Please research some of the names that we mentioned, like Congo Square, house music, disco music, etc. It's important to me, it's important to our country, and as we're exporting this to everywhere else, it's important to understand where it came from.

# Carl Schmidt

**Carl Schmidt** is a Business Education teacher at Monte Vista High School in Cupertino, California. He is one of the founders of Silicon Valley DECA, one of three California Districts. He just ended his second term as Chairperson of the California Association of DECA.

Mr. Schmidt completed his undergraduate work in Economics and later earned both a Masters Of Business Administration (International Business) and a Master of Arts in Education (Educational Leadership). Prior to his teaching career, he was a senior consultant for Price Waterhouse in New York City and both a Manager, Information Systems and Materials Manager for Xerox Corporation's Southern California Manufacturing Operations. He also had the opportunity to serve as a co-founder and Executive Vice President of a Global Electronics start-up.

# American Culture

Transcribed by: Allen Bryan/Edward Bryan

We will cover some of the key elements of American culture, including:

- Opportunity

- American Exceptionalism

- Mythology

- Right to Bear Arms

- Manifest Destiny

- Pluralism

- The Business of America

- Education

- Creative Destruction

- Federalism and Election

Hopefully, we will challenge some of the previous understandings you may have. First, let us look at "opportunity". This is the reason we have successive waves of immigrants coming to America. There's a promise of life, liberty, and the pursuit of happiness. We say that there are four freedoms we believe in: freedom of speech, freedom of worship, freedom from want, and freedom from fear. So, immigrants came for many reasons: economic reasons, religious persecution, political persecution or just to find a new way of life. In America, there was a tremendous amount of land and there was an opportunity for the dispossessed of the world to create and build wealth. We all have heard the story, the Horatio Alger myth, that America is inherently different from other nations. We were the first democracy since ancient Greece. We believe in the vision of America as a city upon a hill, a biblical reference. We believe in liberty, egalitarianism, individualism, republicanism, democracy, and of course laissez faire - little or no interference by the government. These are the classic American images, all part of our mythology. Our mythology also consists of the belief that any immigrant coming to our shores can move from rags to riches. All that is required is to lead an exemplary life and struggle valiantly against poverty and adversity, gain wealth and honor and realize the "American Dream". Freedom and wealth and individualism - that is the "American Dream". When our founding fathers created the Declaration of Independence from Britain, there was a reason why we created that separation. Whenever a form of government becomes destructive of those ends, life, liberty, and the pursuit of happiness, it is the right of the people to alter or abolish it and institute a new government. That was the foundation of our own revolution.

Those principles of July 4, 1776, were enshrined in something we call the Constitution of the United States. That Constitution was an agreement among all of the 13 original colonies which became the states. They formed the constitution, but that constitution was not going to be ratified or approved unless we had something called a Bill of Rights, which consisted of 10 amendments to the constitution. The first amendment is the freedom of speech and expression. The second is the right to bear arms. George Washington said that free people should not only be armed and disciplined, but they should have sufficient arms and ammunition to maintain a status of independence from any who would attempt to abuse them, which would include their own government. This was not a right exclusive to men. There are many statues in New England showing revolutionary-era women carrying arms. This idea has led to the current environment in the United States, which has more weapons per person than any other country in the world (120.5 weapons per 100 citizens).

Next, we want to talk about manifest destiny or the idea that America was destined to expand. The thirteen original colonies expanded by people moving ever westward. In 1783, after a war of independence from Britain, we got larger. Then in 1803, we acquired land from France, through an agreement with Napoleon Bonaparte. This was called the Louisiana Purchase. Napoleon thought that if America grew, it would eventually be a rival to England, which was France's greatest enemy. Florida was acquired from Spain, and then Texas, which had become an independent country, was annexed into America. Further west, the U.S. acquired the southwest from Mexico. Then the Oregon territory was taken after negotiations with Britain.

We believe in pluralism and we are a nation of immigrants. Every one of us or our ancestors is from another region of the world. Even the native peoples are believed to have traversed a land bridge to come to the American continents. There was a push-pull system, meaning there were reasons pushing people out of their homeland and there is the pull of opportunity which brought them here. Most immigrant groups have joined America by chain migration. An individual, typically a male would come here first. Then he would get a job, find some way to improve his life and gain enough money to bring his family members over. Our national model here is the Latin phrase "E Pluribus Unum" - from many ones. Here, of course, you will see part of our mythology again, the melting pot. The idea of the melting pot says all these people from different parts of the world become American. In many parts of the world, such as Europe, people differentiate each other by racial, cultural, and ethnic identity. The same is true for Asia and Africa, however, in the United States, you cannot look at a person's ethnicity or culture and say you are American. We could be American regardless of our ancestry or birth. That is the concept of the melting pot. So, we have people from China, Russia, Italy, Mexico, Germany, Britain, Ireland, etc. You can name the country; they have come to America and have become Americans. A map from the 2000 census that looks at the counties of each state shows the major ethnicity in each county. You see French, Hispanic, African, Scotch Irish, German, etc. There is even one county that is majority Chinese - San Francisco.

Now we move on to creative destruction. It is inherent in capitalism. One form of capitalism will always replace another. It is an incessant innovation mechanism where new production units replace outdated ones. It's a process of industrial mutation that incessantly revolutionizes the economic structure from within. So, nothing is going to be static in a Capitalist environment. Right now, we have major companies such as Amazon, Tesla, etc. Jeff Bezos says that one day even Amazon will go bankrupt. Some other company will replace it. What is the business of America? Frankly, "the business of America is business". That was said by president Calvin Coolidge. No other country says its purpose is business. If we are going to have a democracy and we are going to have people self-governing, we are going to need education if our primary national output is business. Thomas Jefferson, who wrote the declaration of independence, said to educate and inform the whole mass of the people. They are the only sure reliance for the preservation of our liberty. Nelson Mandela said that education is the most powerful weapon which you can use to change the world and we have a shrine in our constitution of the United States and in our states that we believe in free appropriate education. We recognized that societies reproduce themselves in only two ways, biologically and culturally. Education is a site of cultural reproduction. John Dewey, one of our education philosophers, shares with us what's the best and wisest parent for his own child. Democracy cannot succeed unless those citizens learn to express their choice or prepare to choose wisely. The real safeguard for democracy, therefore, is education -

Franklin Roosevelt our 32nd president.

At the top of the hierarchy of democracy is public education. To sustain democracy, we need critical thinking skills, creative thinking skills, and lifelong learning. These not only help preserve democracy but also support business. All of this together provides a curriculum and instruction, which influences teachers and students. The United States was perhaps the first country to understand the need for business education. This first started at the University of Pennsylvania, where the Wharton school of business was founded. Wharton believed we needed business classes at the college and doctoral levels. A business education includes leadership and managerial skills, communication skills, time management skills, business ethics, etc.

Now, the final cornerstone of democracy is free and fair elections. We have seen pictures of former president Bill Clinton and his wife Hillary attending Donald Trump's wedding to Melania many years ago. Presumably, the Clintons were friends and honored guests of the Trumps at that time. Moving ahead to 2016, Trump and Hillary Clinton are opposing each other for the presidency. At this time, they each made it clear that each did not like the other policies or even as people. Later, Trump was later unseated by Joe Biden. It is free and fair elections that separate us from dictatorships. George Washington, our first president set the first example of how a presidency should be transitioned to prevent the installation of a monarchy or dictatorship. Currently, we have a two-party system that gives a choice of governing philosophies. This allows viewpoints to be counterbalanced and negotiations to occur to find the best solution for the country. The allowance for varied viewpoints gives resilience to our government. The checks and balances provided by the different branches of government (executive, legislative, judiciary) serve as a buffer to one branch, or person, from gaining too much power. This allows the democratic system to bend with ideological winds without breaking.

# Dr. Jay Jones

**Dr. Jay Jones** has a broad academic background, with concentrations in Botany, Microbiology, Chemistry, and Geology. His research and work experience includes Senior Research Geobotanist, conducting research on oil and gas exploration (ARCO), Naturalist/Interpreter (National Park Service), and Remote Sensing Consultant (NASA/Lockheed). He is currently in the field conducting floral surveys, as well as in the laboratory working with complex analytical instrumentation. As Professor of Biology and Biochemistry, Jones has taught an exceptionally broad range of courses including versions of an interdisciplinary course entitled: Toward a Sustainable Planet. Many of these courses have field components in which faculty and students see the global impact of the human species in various countries around the world.

# Higher Education

Transcribed by: Yiming (Amelia) Wang

We have talked about our democracy, the maintenance of our well-being, and the common good. Education is a prime key to a better world for the future. I will talk about the view of education, the different pathways you can take, and each individual has certain needs, talents, and so forth, so different paths are good for different people.

Most people seek higher education to get a job, and the motivation is to do well financially, and to have a higher level of prestige, so they have higher degrees in education. But few enter college simply with a passion to learn. But college really needs to Broaden one's understanding of the world around us, help you become a more informed global citizen, prepare you to be able to lead a quality life given the global challenges ahead, enhance your ability to contribute to the "common good", and help you understand and be able to meet the challenges of the Anthropocene. Education today must have elements to help you fit with the changing world today.

When you get to college, you are away from family and get to learn new things, religions, and people. You are educated in different disciplines, and they help you to understand the world around you. In many cases, they change your view of the world, and in some cases, even your values.

I was able to become an SRA (Student Recruitment Ambassador) and worked closely with the faculty. I explored 3 different majors and general education really opened my eyes. I could see many opportunities in the world. I wanted to be a pharmacist, entering college to pursue that profession, but learned there was much more than that. After exploring many opportunities, I no longer wanted to be a pharmacist. This is just an illustration of what college is for me, a fantastic world out there with different music, religion, culture, reality, and politics. It was like opening up a window of a home with a limited view. It's important to understand that education occurs not only in classrooms and labs, it occurs as you are immersed in the college. You learn from seminars and the community that you are in.

Being exposed to art and literature, and just talking with other students about philosophy–all of these are extracurricular learning opportunities. When you are studying, remember to take some time out and explore nature. Spending some time out in nature reduces stress. General education courses may not be directly related to your professional future, but are exceedingly important to develop your understanding of a citizen of the world and nation. It is important to understand government, history, etc., and to have a broad education beyond the specific professions. It is important to consider values, which are critically important in contributing to the common good, we have destructive and constructive values. Education programs should at least expose the importance of values. Point out the importance, but not necessarily dictate those values. Travel can be an important component, getting out of your own country, and seeing what the world is like. These are some places where I have taken students.

Choosing a college or university–there are many different colleges, and choosing a specific one is extremely important. Some are very expensive, some are almost free, some are best for super achievers, who will benefit from competitive environments, and these are schools like the University of Chicago, Harvard, etc. There are other schools that second-degree students will benefit from more, where they are more focused on education, and not necessarily research. In choosing a college you have to decide what you want from college, is it the reputation, or is it the quality of the program? Many of the best programs or disciplines are not at the top lane of big names. So, you have to figure out what you want out of your college education.

These are the major types of colleges, community colleges, traditional 4-year undergrad, and those with advanced degrees like master's programs. State colleges are generally less expensive, they have larger classes, and institutions are larger in terms of enrollment and class size than private institutions. The doctoral learning institutions get a lot of money from research overhead, and they are not as concerned about education, but rather scholarly work. For an undergrad student, going into a research-intensive college may not be the best choice. They may thrive better in an environment focused on undergraduate education. Whereas, other students may benefit from the environment of a college with advanced degree programs, which allow you to have access to research opportunities. They each offer different ways for each student to achieve optimal learning.

Most private institutions are non-profit, but there are some colleges and universities specifically designed to make money. Some of these are legitimate schools, but they pay faculties poorly, and they do not offer good quality programs. We all see that much education is occurring online, as the pandemic rages, many of us still go to online institutions or programs. But it's having a devastating effect in many institutions, especially in sciences, where laboratories are not hands-on. Many of my colleagues have complained about such cases.

Education should prepare you for the changes that are going on right now. It is very clear that we need a paradigm shift in both our economic systems and our lifestyle systems. In many places in the world, the structure is now falling apart, and we in the developed world will see an increasing disruption both environmentally, economically, and socially. Unfortunately, most schools have not incorporated this element of learning.

Let me conclude by saying my education has been the most valuable aspect of my life. I cannot think of anything in my life that has a greater value than the education that I received.

# Siqi Li

**Siqi Li** is a senior at Gulliver Preparatory in Florida. Her hobbies are art and reading, she is also interested in art, sociology, and psychology.

## Art in Protest

What art is meant to do is a question that can be answered in various ways, but today I want to focus on art and its place in social movements and protests. First, it is important to talk about what protest art is. Protest art, or activist art, generally goes against the grain. Instead of describing or representing the status quo, they challenge it. They "form [...] political or social currency [and] actively [address] cultural power structures" (Tate, 2022). This can take the form of paintings, posters, banners, and other printed materials as well as performances, graffiti and street art, and installations. The art itself does not create change, but rather encourages and emboldens people to mobilize for a cause. These art forms, some extremely accessible to everyone, emerged upon the call to create space for marginalized and disenfranchised communities to be heard. Thus, you have probably seen protest art having subjects like Black Lives Matter, feminism, the AIDs crisis, immigration, and many more.

You might've seen Picasso's *Guernica*, a very famous painting done by a very famous artist. This 1937 oil painting is often regarded as one of Picasso's most well-known works, but also a powerful anti-war image, depicting the bombing of the village of Guernica during the Spanish Civil War. The painting itself is in no way realistic, the black and white, cubist depiction of the atrocities shows the brutality of war and an assault on humanity (Nicole Dean, 2022). Diego Rivera, one of the leaders of the 1920s Mexican Mural Movement, was also someone that actively created protest art. Choosing murals as his primary medium as opposed to the traditional canvas that could be displayed in a gallery, he protested against the ruling class, the church, capitalism, etc. (Ruth Millington, 2020). Choosing to paint large-scale murals on public walls was also a deliberate decision, making it more accessible to his audience: the working class.

While working on a local campaign in response to President Jimmy Carter's Immigration Plan, Yolanda López created the iconic poster "Who's the Illegal Alien, Pilgrim?" (Google Arts & Culture,

2022). The poster depicts an Aztec soldier in the famous Uncle Sam pose. Contrary to other posters that clad the slogan "No Human Being is Illegal"', López's statement chose a different narrative, taking on a more authoritative tone, reminding the audience of the history of European colonization of the Americas (political graphics, 2021). I also want to focus on some specific artists when talking about protest art. These are artists who, in my opinion, have large bodies of work focusing on activism. Though this is not to say some aforementioned artists, like Diego Rivera and Yolanda López, do not have protest pieces.

The first one I want to talk about is Guerrilla Girls. Established in 1985 in New York City, the Guerrilla Girls were a group of anonymous feminist female artists who protested and fought against the lack of recognition and for the inclusion of women in the art world. Wearing gorilla masks and using the names of deceased female artists as pseudonyms, they focused on gender and racial inequalities in the art world (Elena Martinique, 2022). "They are most well-known for clever and humorous posters, billboards, flyers and books which criticize large publicly funded institutions and private galleries for their lack of pay, and inclusion for marginalized artists" (Ruth Millington, 2020). The second artist I'm going to talk about is Keith Haring. You might have seen pictures/drawings of his famous dancing figures, but his work reaches beyond that. Haring was prominent in the

New York art scene in the 1980s and was an active activist during that time. He often created art that addressed socially important issues, such as the AIDs crisis, apartheid in South Africa, LGBTQ+ rights, the Cold War, and the military-industrial complex, with his pop art style making his artwork and message accessible and memorable. At the end of the day, art is political, art is social. Art creates and supports communities. Art is a tool of resistance. I want to end this presentation with a quote by Ai Weiwei: "If anything, art is... about morals, about our belief in humanity. Without that, there simply is no art."

# Allen Bryan

**Allen Bryan** is an 11th-grade student at Junipero Serra High school in California. He is interested in the STEM and pre-med fields. He is starting his own Pre-med club to help students at his school gain knowledge and interest in science, as well as finding opportunities for them, such as internships. He also expresses his love for music through his school Jazz Band and classical music playing. He also plays football and runs track for his school.

## American Football

Football is a very American sport, but it has its roots in variations of rugby and soccer that were played in the 1800s. Intercollegiate matches became popular in the late 1800s and in 1875 Harvard and Yale played the first intercollegiate match of a game that was then most similar to rugby. A Yale undergrad, and later medical student, Walter Camp, was instrumental in changes to the game and its rules. Camp is known as the "Father of American Football". This style of football grew in popularity and spread to other colleges and high schools across the United States. In 1920 a professional football league was created, which later became the National Football League (NFL). Football is now the most popular spectator sport in America, with more fans than baseball, which is known as the American pastime.

What is football? To Americans, this question might seem funny, since it is the most watched sport in America. To oversimplify, football is a sport where two teams compete to score points by taking a ball across the opponent's goal line. The team in possession of the football is called the offense. The team without the ball is the defense and tries to defend its goal line. For various reasons, the defense can take possession of the ball and then become the offense. The other team then becomes the defense.  Each player on each team has a role to play. For example, a quarterback controls the ball and can hand it off another player, throw it (pass it) to another player, or run it himself. Receivers catch and run the ball. Offensive linemen protect their man carrying the ball. Defensive linemen attempt to prevent the offense from moving forward with the ball. The details of each position are more than can be explained here.

My journey in football began when I was in junior high school. My friends and I would always talk about the San Francisco 49ers, our local pro football team. We would read about them, watch the games, and imagine making the plays. Pro players are fast and strong and use their skills to take the ball, score points, win the game, and become sports heroes. It was exciting and I wanted to be part of this sport. I was happy to find that my choice of high school, Junipero Serra, had one of the top football programs in the state of California and had a history of developing great ball players. One of them is Tom Brady, the greatest quarterback to ever play the game. In my freshman year at Serra, I joined the junior varsity (JV) football team and became a Serra Padre, the Padre being the school symbol. Unfortunately, there were many boys with more experience, so I did not get much playing time that year. The JV coaches, however, helped me to learn the game and find a position that best suited me - defensive end. As a defensive end, you are usually one of the first through the line of scrimmage to take down the quarterback and simultaneously one of the last lines of defense in preventing the other team from scoring. You have to not only cover your position in the backfield and guard your opposing player but anticipate where the other team will take the ball and find or make opportunities to take the ball from them. In the offseason, I ran, lifted weights, and watched videos of football games to better learn my role on the team. By my sophomore year, I felt ready. I was bigger, stronger, and hopefully more knowledgeable. At the beginning of the season, I still did not get much playing time, but as the coaches began to trust me and see how much I had improved, they gave me more and more playing time. By the end of the season, I was a starting player and felt that I had made a great contribution to our winning season and league title. I was now ready to move up to varsity, where the struggle to be a key contributor will begin again. No matter what happens, however, I know that football has given me more than I could ever give back. I have learned a lot about hard work and developing confidence, but more importantly, I have learned about team spirit and making friendships that will last a lifetime.

My experience is not unique. The benefits of a sport like football are multitude and can positively affect the lives of the teenagers playing. Football, like many other sports, has great health benefits, such as improving cardiovascular capacity and increasing physical strength. You develop a work ethic, setting high standards and developing the discipline to meet and exceed them. You learn teamwork by working with others to achieve goals. Through football, you are taught leadership by learning from those who come before you and guiding those who come after. But football is a time-consuming sport and to excel both in it and in school, you will have to learn time management skills. Through shared sacrifice in adverse situations, you will also build camaraderie and lifelong friendships. Finally, high school football can be very helpful in applying for college.

Universities place a high value on great football teams, because successful teams generate huge profits, while most other sports lose money. One financial website (Businessinsider.com, 2017) reported that football brings in an average of $31.9 million dollars per college per year. This money is used to cover the cost of sports facilities, coaching, and scholarships. Successful programs make enough to pay for unprofitable sports. Some schools may cover all or part of your tuition and living expenses if you play football for them. By the NCAA rules, football can provide 10-20 times the number of scholarships as most other sports. Unfortunately, Ivy League schools do not give sports scholarships. But having good grades and being recruited to play a sport can almost guarantee acceptance to the school of your dreams. Even if you are not recruited to play college football, participating in the sport in high school can help bolster your extracurricular activities list. It can show leadership, teamwork, and discipline. These are things colleges look for when selecting applicants.

In conclusion, football is part of the American experience. In the United States, football is the top spectator sport. During football season, you are likely to find the average American attending or watching games on a regular basis. Over 100 million watches the Super Bowl, the final pro game of the season.  Keeping up with your favorite team makes you feel like a part of a community. You come to work or school on Monday morning ready to talk about the big game from the past weekend or the upcoming game next week. You don't have to play the game to enjoy it, but playing the game can help you build fitness and a strong work ethic, as well as leadership and time management skills.

# Owen Ouyang

**Owen Ouyang** is a rising 11th grader (A1 in the A-level curriculum) who attends Shenzhen College of International Education, Kwangtung. He's keen on arts, history, politics, and philosophies. He enjoys reading in his spare time.

## Politicization of Aesthetics

The politicization of aesthetics is the idea that art is often incorporated into and subjugated for political ends. It is rare that you will find political artwork that is neutral. For example, a painting of Bill Clinton and Monica Lewinsky, with Clinton holding two guns and a flying American flag at the back, is clearly political satire. Soviet-era propaganda posters clearly show healthy, strong young men and women with hammers and sickles raised, indicating solidarity with the purposes of the state. Fascism has also employed art. The Italian fascist dictator, Benito Mussolini, used it before and during the Second World War, often depicting him as a strong leader, a tool used by leaders even today. Even political artwork that seems neutral, may not be. That form of art was called 'socialist realism, and it was the official form of art in Stalin's Russia. It portrays the scene of the ideal life of the proletariat as an embodiment of the 'communist utopia'. So primarily, it was used as Soviet state propaganda. To make people believe that the communists are devoting themselves to such an ideal course

If we are going to investigate the politicization of aesthetics, we have to first, understand aesthetics without politics. In 1790, Immanuel Kant (1724-1804) published his renowned work — *Critique of the Power of Judgment*. According to Kant, aesthetic judgment should be subjective and speak with a single, universal voice. From this, he then coined the notion of disinterestedness, in which he openly assumed the role of extrinsic considerations such as political or utilitarian concerns plays in the appreciation of beauty was to be only provoking conflicts. In his argument, artworks should be viewed as objects. And Every object has to be conceived in a twofold manner: first as an appearance, subject to the necessary jurisdiction of certain basic concepts (i.e., the Categories in Kantian philosophy) and to the forms of space and time; second, as a thing in itself, about which nothing more can be said.

If you take a thorough look, Kant was very idealistic and somewhat against human nature. Because, when we analyze every artwork, we cling to some settings off the scene. For instance, in the work of Vincent Van Gogh, we often highlight his personal experience and usually take into account his psychopathic tendencies, that he attempted to commit suicide multiple times and, ultimately, ended up killing himself. So, in appreciation of his work, we often take these factors into consideration. But Kant taught us, NO, an artwork is an artwork per se, an artwork is an artwork in itself, rather than the woven of certain personal experience whatever political moral or anything else, an artwork is an artwork in itself. And such extrinsic considerations of artwork are simply messing around. The various themes of Kant's *Critique of Judgment* have had a major impact over the two centuries since its publication. For example, the accounts of brilliance and the importance of imagination in aesthetics became the basis of Romanticism in the early 19th century. Also, a movement inspired by him was the French Aesthetics Movement, sometimes called 'the art for art's sake' movement. The 'art for art's sake' movement, was inspired by Immanuel Kant, and simultaneously by many other great thinkers at the time, of course. The beautiful, for Emmanuel Kant, is "that which without any concept is cognized as the object of necessary satisfaction." That is, the appropriate attitude of the viewer to perceive "beauty" is that of 'indifference.' Because by nature, you should be satisfied when you take the first glimpse of the artwork.

"Art for the art's sake" became a bohemian creed in the 19th century; a slogan raised in defiance of those—from John Ruskin, an artist in the Victorian era, to the much contemporary Communist advocates of the so-called socialist realism—who share the ideological similarities that the value of art was to serve some moral or didactic purpose. It was a rejection of the Marxist aim of politicizing art. Art for the sake of art affirmed that intrinsically, artworks are valuable as arts in themselves, that artistic pursuits were their own justification.

James Whistler said 'Art should be independent of all claptrap – should stand alone...and appeal to the artistic sense of eye or ear, without confounding this with emotions entirely foreign to it, as devotion, pity, love, patriotism and the like." But whence did the politicization of aesthetics come from? The stories began with Friedrich Nietzsche, who claimed that there is 'no art for art's sake'. In his renowned 'Twilight to the Idols', he argued: "When the purpose of moral preaching and of improving man has been excluded from art, it still does not follow by any means that art is altogether purposeless, aimless, senseless — in short, l'art pour l'art, a worm chewing its own tail. "Rather no purpose at all than a moral purpose!" — that is the talk of mere passion. A psychologist, on the other hand, asks: what does all art do? Does it not praise? Glorify? Choose? Prefer? With all this, it strengthens or weakens certain valuations. Is this merely a "moreover"? An accident? Something in which the artist's instinct had no share? Or is it not the very presupposition of the artist's ability? Does his basic instinct aim at art, or rather at the sense of art, at life? at the desirability of life? Art is the great stimulus to life: how could one understand it as purposeless, as aimless, as arts only for the arts sake?"

Well, Nietzsche was kind of famous for his superman ethics, the Uber mensch, and became notorious after a century due to his ideological affinity with fascism. And the first fascist leader, Benito Mussolini, immensely subscribed to aesthetics. His commitment to aesthetics ensured that symbols, art, and rituals were all seen as contributing to a transformative, molding power. They straightforwardly informed how Mussolini envisioned and exercised his power. Mussolini subscribed to the aesthetics promoted by the art for art's sake movement, that is, the notion of art as autonomous and self-referential and detached from worldly matters. At the same time, and somewhat paradoxically, Mussolini had a great intuition about the pivotal role of sensation, of emotion in politics. This intuition, combined with his approach to aesthetics, gave way to the strange and lethal alchemy that we know as fascism.

As Mussolini envisaged, for politics not to be a filthy word that inexorably connotes to the failing political class's capacity, embodied in endless debates and conservatism, it had to play a role much more bold and proactive; politics was supposed to change how actually live and think in the society. The issue was not only about shifts in the government: the cliche of political compromises and formulas. With fascism, the goal was to revolutionize the meaning of politics itself in order to construct a new Italy on the ruins of the old one.

Here is where the idea of the politician as the artist comes in.

The artist politician destroys in order to create, as doctor Carl Schmitt just mentioned, creative destruction. "Molding," "sculpting," and "shaping" were terms that became popular in Mussolini's discourse when he referred to the masses and their transformation into ideal fascist models. Politics was an art for Mussolini, and he liked to think of himself as a sculptor who alone could render hard material into malleable constructions, into pliable artifacts. Is there anything more radical in terms of disregard for people, than this approach that dehumanizes people as materials? – it is an approach that exactly defines totalitarianism.

Mussolini's style and emphasis changed over the years, but Mussolini's central position in the fascist constellation was unwavering and unrivaled. Indeed, it is even constantly growing and gaining attention, attributed to the media's ability to convey Mussolini's image through traditional printed press, cinema, and the radio. From the lion tamer to the rural worker, motorcyclist, father, and commander, Mussolini's figure affirmed fascism's value and helped build fascism as a longstanding regime. Twenty years - not an insignificant stretch of time.

So here comes the analysis of Walter Benjamin, a prominent figure in the Frankfurt school. When it comes to the aestheticization of politics, the evocative and disturbing image Benjamin conjured to make his argument was the comparison of bombed-out sites in Ethiopia, which as a rather pre-modern nation, was by the time suffering Italian colonization, to the blooming flowers on the ruin. For Benjamin, such an image implied an aestheticized view of violence and war, of destruction and pain, an artistic transfiguration that overcame bodily material reality For Benjamin, the paradox was what he called 'the age of mechanical reproduction'. Art, when politicized, became one that made people feel minuscule and in awe of authority, which eventually ended up instead becoming an instrument of domination.

Fascism's aesthetic politics does not imply that all connections between aesthetics and politics are pernicious; they are not necessarily bad. But it demonstrates the high potential of growing into an apparatus of radicalism. Aesthetics, in sum, does not necessarily derive from fascist or authoritarian outcomes. But we need to make some distinctions, especially when it comes to the question of the affective and emotional side of aesthetic politics. We cannot leave the monopoly over expressive politics to those who abuse it.

# Andy Dai

**Andy Dai** is a student at the Affiliated School of JNU for Hong Kong & Macao Students. In school/study life, his hobbies are economics and sports, and he serves as the captain of the school basketball team.

## Exercise for high school students

I am a student at the Affiliated School of JNU for Hong Kong & Macao Students, where I serve as the captain of the school basketball team. In today's society, we have access to many different types of sports activities in school. I believe in the benefits of sports and exercise. Exercise can help correct bad character and weaknesses by providing a structured environment in which to develop discipline and team spirit. A happy sports experience is a way of educating yourself and building character. Participation in sports builds habits that can help you achieve lifelong aspirations. Participation can improve cardiopulmonary function and alleviate the pressure of study. It can build team spirit through competition. There are many sports in our schools and finding the one that motivates you can strengthen the body, also increase learning efficiency, and create a well-rounded human being.

# Suri Zheng

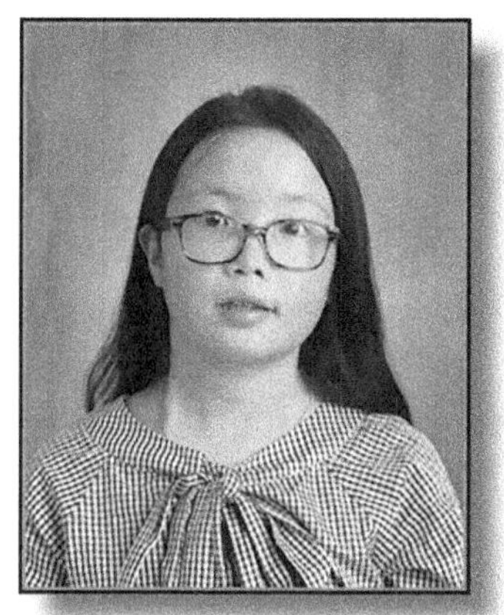

**Suri Zheng** is an incoming sophomore at Palo Alto High School (Paly). Her hobbies include doing arts and crafts, hanging out with her friends, and playing the piano.

## Tipping Customs in America

### Tipping Customs in America

The average tipping amount is 20% of your bill, but that can vary depending on the service given. For example, people might give more tips if the food was exceptionally good or less if it took a long time for the food to arrive.

### Tipping Habits of Americans

20% is the average tipping amount in America and it's polite to give tips especially when the waiter or waitress depends on the tips, But there are some examples where people don't give any tips. In a recent survey, 70% of waiters and waitresses said they had not received tips in their years of working.

### Tipping Based on Gender

In a recent survey done on Discover.com, they found out women tip more than men. Reasons range from free food to being attracted to the server.

### Annoying tippers: The party that has too many people

The tipping rule is giving 20% or more of your bill, but there are some people that always go under. In this case, a waitress was serving a table with 26 people! And of course, serving 26 people was already hard enough adding on that the waitress printed out 26 individual bills for the customers because they wanted to pay for their own meals. The check came out to be $500 but the tips added together by those 26 people were only $10!

### Generous tips

Sometimes there are some people that go above and beyond their tipping. Like the singer, Taylor Swift. In 2013, after a concert in PA, Swift treated her 18 staff as well as Austin Mahone and Ed Sheeran to an Italian meal at a local Philly restaurant. The pop star ended up leaving a whooping $500 tip on an $800 bill.

# Yisha Tang

**Yisha Tang** is a student at the Shenzhen College of International Education. I love biology, computer science, and traditional cultures. Today, I will introduce a traditional culture of China--the tea culture in China.

## Chinese Tea Culture

China is the origin of tea culture. Chinese tea culture originated from the Shennong family in ancient times. It has a history of more than 4,700 years. In ancient books and documents. It is recorded that "Shen Nong tasted all kinds of herbs, encountered twelve poisons every day, and use tea as antidotes". Chinese tea culture started in ancient times, but tea was used as a drink in the period of Lu Zhougong. After entering the Tang Dynasty, the habit of drinking tea gradually became popular, and it entered a prosperous period in the Song Dynasty. During the Ming and Qing Dynasties, the varieties of tea became more and more abundant, and the tea-drinking method also developed. In the 20th century, with the development of trade, India, Sri Lanka, Indonesia, and other countries introduced tea seeds from China for production and cultivation.

Regarding the origin of the word tea, according to the "Book of Songs" and other relevant documents, in early history, "tea" generally refers to various bitter wild plant foods. The independent word "tea" originated in the Han dynasty, after the discovery of its medicinal value and drinking value. The academy agrees that tea production began in Sichuan. The Sichuan region is deep inland, with low terrain, and surrounded by mountains. It has always been in areas with frequent diseases and plagues. The special regional and natural conditions determining people's dietary customs encourage Sichuan people to drink tea to prevent diseases brought by miasma. Tea is also used as an antidote. The spiritual connotation of tea culture is a cultural phenomenon with distinctive Chinese cultural characteristics formed by the combination of habits such as making tea, appreciating tea, smelling tea, drinking tea, and tasting tea with Chinese cultural connotations and etiquette. So, drinking tea is also a ritual.

According to the color and processing method of tea, there are six types of tea in China: green tea, black tea, oolong tea, white tea, dark tea, and yellow tea.

Green tea is the most produced type of tea in China, and it is unfermented tea. After the fresh leaves are spread and dried, they are directly fried in a hot pot of two or three hundred degrees to maintain their green color. Because the leaves and broth are green, it is called green tea. Green tea has the characteristics of high aroma, mellow taste, and beautiful shape.

Black tea is the exact opposite of green tea and is a fully fermented tea (fermentation degree greater than 80%). Because of its red leaves and broth, it is called black tea. Black tea is withered during processing so that the fresh leaves lose part of their moisture, and then rolled and fermented to oxidize the tea polyphenols contained in them and turn them into red compounds. This compound is partly soluble in water, partly insoluble in water, and accumulates in the leaves, thereby forming red broth and red leaves.

Oolong tea belongs to the semi-fermented tea category. It is produced after picking, withering, shaking, frying, rolling, and baking. The production of it combines the features of the production of both black tea and green tea. White tea belongs to the category of slightly fermented tea, which is processed after drying or simmering without rolling.

White tea has a natural fragrance. Among white tea, the white tea with white hair and silver color is the most valuable. The broth color is slightly yellow and the taste is sweet and mellow. The main producing areas are Fuding City and Zhenghe County, Fujian Province.

Dark tea belongs to the category of post-fermented tea, which is oily black or dark brown due to the long fermentation time. Dark tea has lipid-lowering, weight-loss, and blood pressure-lowering effects.

Yellow tea belongs to the category of slightly fermented tea. It has yellow leaves and yellow soup, hence the name of it is yellow tea. Yellow tea is divided into three categories: "yellow bud tea", "yellow small tea" and "yellow big tea". The production method of yellow tea is a bit like green tea, but the process of yellowing is required in the middle, but green tea is not fermented, while yellow tea belongs to the category of fermented tea.

Reasons for Drinking Tea

1. Tea can lift people's spirits and enhance their thinking and memory abilities.

2. Tea can eliminate fatigue and promote metabolism.

3. Drinking tea is very good for preventing dental caries.

4. Tea contains many trace elements that are beneficial to the human body.

5. Tea has the effect of inhibiting malignant tumors, and drinking tea can significantly inhibit the growth of cancer cells.

6.  Drinking tea can inhibit cell aging and prolong life.

7.  Drinking tea can excite the central nervous system and enhance exercise ability.

8.  Drinking tea has good weight loss and beauty effects.

9.  Drinking tea can prevent senile cataracts.

10. Drinking tea can protect human hematopoietic function.

11. Drinking tea can prevent heatstroke.

**Winford Chang**

**Winford Chang** is a 15-year-old student in Las Vegas, Nevada. Currently, he is attending A-Tech High School as a computer science major. He has many hobbies which include cooking, football, martial arts, and guitar. In his free time, he loves to hang out with friends and work out.

# Cultural Foods

Cultures around the globe all have many different aspects of entertainment, religion, and most of all food. Food is an essential part of every culture around the world. There are no two cultures in the world that have the exact same dishes and meals, and an important part of every culture's food is fast food. Whether in a hurry or just too tired to make food, fast food will almost always hit the spot. And many cultures have different styles for their fast food. Right now, we're going to look at China and America. Both of these countries have lots of variety in the way they serve fast food and even more variety in the fast food itself.

Fast food in America is commonly served in restaurants and usually a little bit more leaning toward the expensive side. The dishes often include food like hamburgers, sandwiches, and fried food although there are still many unique fast-food options in America such as seafood, drinks, and many more. Many fast-food options in America take inspiration from other cultures. Examples are Chipotle which takes inspiration from Hispanic culture, and Panda Express which takes ideas from Chinese cuisine. Fast food restaurants are usually found scattered around cities and have established companies while fast food in China is usually found in the form of street food. The serving sizes are large and amazingly cheap. The food is usually handmade and served on the spot. Food like grilled kebabs, fried food, and dishes like soup dumplings and rice are also extremely common. The street food stalls are usually run by individuals and families. Although neither is the healthiest form of food, they are both great for a fast option while in a hurry. An American option similar to the Chinese street vendors is the food trucks that spread across cities each day. These trucks contain cooking facilities that make freshly cooked food available to offices and neighborhoods across America.

Although some may say that one is better, in reality, both should be appreciated for the certain role that they play. They enable cheaper and faster options of food for people of all classes. With the rise of fast food in recent years, we are not even close to the end of fast food and many new possibilities are still yet to arise and excitement for new fast-food chains and vendors is at an all-time high.

# Yaxuan Yang

**Yaxuan Yang** is a sophomore at Millburn High School in New Jersey. She likes reading and singing in her free time.

## Differences in Lifestyle Between America and China

My experience in living in China until the second grade, moving to America, returning to China for the fifth and sixth grades, and then returning to America, makes me uniquely suited to describing the many lifestyle differences in these two countries.

I'd like to start off by talking about dishes in China and America. Growing up, I remember times that our family would gather and share the dishes of food with each other. When we went out to eat, we'd always order food and share the food. However, after moving to America, I found eating to be a completely different concept. Westerners always ordered their own servings and enjoyed their individual dish. They rarely shared. It's very interesting to see the different cultures among America and China. I, myself, do not stick to a certain type; I like to adapt based on my surroundings.

Along with the topic of meals, I'd like to talk about water. I'll start off by talking about China. Growing up, I'd always be given cups of warm water to drink at any event, for example, family gatherings, a friend's birthday party, or even just a glass of warm water for breakfast. I was taught that boiling water was better for the digestive system and for my own health. I was also told that boiling water would kill bacteria that may be in tap water, so I spent most of my years drinking warm water. After moving to America, I noticed myself asking for warm water in restaurants and boiling water at home. When I went to the house of a friend of mine, she handed me cold water directly from her faucet and drank it all up while I stared at her in silence. I was shocked at how she managed to drink the water when it was 30 degrees outside. It was interesting to see how the two different cultures have such different ways of drinking water. In China, tea also was a huge factor in culture. I remember I used to take classes that taught us how to make tea: Cha Dao. There were specific instructions on which hand to use and which step comes first.  Arriving in America, I just found myself consuming coke, store-bought beverages, and coffee which is made in a coffee machine.

In my opinion, I have a very different perception surrounding communication. In China, I had always found myself to be indirect and I had to think deeply before I talked. Not only did this happen around strangers, but it also happened with my relatives and my teachers at school, or basically anyone older than me. When I moved to America, I found myself thinking about how directly Americans may speak. I felt that they were very casual and upfront with their words, unlike Chinese people, which I found to be seen as more "respectful" and "cautious." For example, in any form of speech, less conflict is seen in Chinese people because they would simply think over their words and ask themselves the question "is it okay for me to say this?", but among Americans, debates may often happen in a conversation until they have reached a mutual agreement.

Next, I want to talk about living in a household in America and China. In China, it is very common for the entire family to be living in the same household. For example, my grandmother and grandfather have lived with their grandson and my aunts in the same household for as long as I can remember. I'd go visit them every weekend and we'd gather as a whole. Commonly, the whole entire family and their generation would live in one big house or apartment. Although that is the case for some American families too, I found most American families to be living in separate households. The grandchildren live on their own, the aunts and uncles live on their own and the grandparents live in their own separate houses too.

Now, I want to ask you all a question. Let's say you go out with a friend and you both arrive at a store full of old antiques. You decide to buy some and go up to the cashier to pay. What payment method would you use? Many people would answer credit card, or cash in America, or even apple pay, which is a plan to solve problems like forgetting your wallet. But a normal Chinese citizen would probably answer with "WeChat, or Alipay. (Weixin and Zhifubao.) They are basically the equivalent of Apple Pay, or even Paypal, Venmo, Zelle, Cash App, etc. In China, stores put out QR codes, making transactions easier, catching up to modern technology and the digital age. It's not just vendors that use this method, according to the insider, the government has implemented the technology into public transportation in many cities in China, which allows people to pay for their fares via QR codes.

Next, I'd like to mention individualism vs collectivism, a concept that is interesting in the discussion of cultural differences in China and America. America has been known for its individualism and for celebrating the individual. The United States is a place in which individuals can shine, while in China society is a group. In China, people's individual accomplishments aren't as important since each person fits into the greater body of the nation. In the United States, people value freedom and individuality. But in China, it is seen as "strange"." Chinese culture places a lot of value on the good of the group as a whole, but in America, it is shown as one person's experience rather than a group. A partial reason is that in China, there are not as many diverse mixes of experiences as in America. In America, walking in the hallways of a school, you could spot many people of different races, and naturally different cultures and experiences.

Last, I'd like to end my presentation by talking about the schooling systems of America and China. In the Chinese education system, in Primary school, there are typically six grades, but in Primary schools in America, there are five instead of six. In China, Junior high school reflects grades

7-9, and year 10-12 is senior high school. In the US, instead of 7-9, Junior high school (middle school) is 6-8 and High School is 9-12. Another difference among the education systems was moving up to another grade. In China, after I had finished 6th grade, it was required for us to take an exam to see which school we'd be accepted into based on our score, but once I moved to America, I realized there was only one public school in my town, and many private schools, so naturally I enrolled in the one and only public school without having to take any exams. While in China, all students need to take an exam in order to go on to middle school or high school, so essentially schools in China have America's private school enrollment process. I want to also mention the process of getting into college. In China, there is an exam called GaoKao, which is a final exam for the 12th graders to take on a certain day. They have to prepare enough so they will pass the test, and that will determine which college they go to. In America, it is completely different. Here instead of a final exam, it is replaced with SAT/ACT scores, a GPA, a college application essay, and more.

In my opinion, China and America's different in many ways. But that's what I think makes the two countries interesting. Studying their lifestyle and culture makes me realize how different the world is. Thank you for listening to my presentation.

# Yiming (Amelia) Wang

**Yiming (Amelia) Wang** is a fourth-year undergraduate student studying at Texas A&M University. She is pursuing a B.S. in Psychology and has a minor in Sociology. Meanwhile, she is also working towards graduate school for a Master's Degree in Industrial-Organizational Psychology. Her future goal is to bring a positive influence on multicultural communities and families. In her free time, Yiming enjoys dancing, cooking, reading, and spending warm afternoons with friends all around.

## Chinese Children's Understanding of Gender & Household Labor

Today I want to talk about an interesting cultural study about Chinese Children's Understanding of Gender and Household Labor.

Prior research has found that women around the world do the vast majority of household labor at home. Prior research with American children has suggested that family structure and larger social context directly influence how children make sense of gender roles within the family. However, despite initial evidence on the important role of larger social context, few studies have focused on exploring how children outside of the US make sense of this gendering of household labor within the family. Therefore, many are wondering how Chinese children make sense of the gendered or often unequal division of household labor.

A total of 35 children from Changchun, an urban center in northern China, were recruited in 2017, including 22 girls and 13 boys with ages ranging from 9 to 12. The children participated in semi-structured interviews conducted in Mandarin, where they were asked both hypothetical and real-world questions about their opinions on gendered labor divisions, such as "under this scenario, do you find the division of chores fair within this family?" "How does that compare to your family?" "If a person is willing to do housework, should he or she be allowed to do more?" "If someone makes more money, should they still do the same amount of housework?" etc.

The children's answers were later transcribed and inductively coded in their original language, which is Mandarin. The purpose of coding is to record what different types of ideas were repeatedly mentioned in the interviews. Examples in this picture are some random codes I picked, such as "Wife uses her expertise to teach husband." or "Young children should do less housework." Usually, once a code has 3 or more supporting examples, it becomes important and is able to reflect what the children are thinking.

So far, it is worth noting that 74.5% reported that their mothers did the majority of household labor at home. 41% believed that the family's distribution shouldn't change. In other words, they recognized it as normality. Most children believe that time availability is the most important factor in housework division, so mothers had more time than fathers, in their opinion.

However, overwhelmingly, children also pointed out how household labor can be divided based on the assumption that men and women have different physical abilities. In this case, since the husband is believed to be physically stronger than his wife, he should be the person to do more housework.

And we have reached the end. What's most fascinating about this cultural study is that unlike data collected from American children who are raised in western culture, it is really fascinating to see how Chinese children choose to accept certain gender stereotypes but apply them to benefit the minority. Thank you so much for your attention.

# US College Panel (edited transcript)

*Albert Zeng, Harvard College Graduate (MC)*

*Ellen Zeng, Harvard Law School Graduate*

*Kevin Bryan, University of Pennsylvania*

*Luis Perez, Stanford Graduate*

*Belinda Zeng, Harvard College Graduate*

*Valerie Morales, UC Irvine*

*Allen Bryan:* Next we would like to introduce our expert panel. This includes Albert Zheng, a Harvard college graduate. Ellen Zheng, a Harvard law school graduate. Kevin Bryan, a student at the University of Pennsylvania. Luis Perez, who is a Stanford graduate. Belinda Zheng, who is a Harvard college graduate, and Valerie Morales who is a University of California Irvine graduate. Thank you so much for being here.

*Albert Zheng:* Alrighty so I'll take that as my queue to enter. As earlier mentioned, my name is Albert, I graduated from Harvard in 2020. I majored in computer science and psychology and since then I've been working as a software engineer at Facebook. So, if the panel members could provide a quick introduction I think that would be helpful so we can match names and faces. So, Ellen, do you want to start us off?

*Ellen Zheng:* Sure, I will start us off. Great, I'm Ellen Zheng. I am a UC Berkeley undergrad, I studied electrical engineering, and computer science as well as a double major. I am also a Harvard Law grad and I am currently a senior strategic operations manager at Splunk.

*Luis Perez:* Hi everyone, I'm Luis. I'm a software engineer at Facebook and I graduated in the class of 2016 from Harvard College. I studied computer science and I received a master's from Stanford in artificial intelligence after that.

*Valerie Morales:* Hi I'm Valerie Morales, I graduated from the University of California Irvine in 2006 and I have extensive experience in the non-profit sector and currently work in the segmentation analytics task.

*Belinda Zheng:* Hey I'm Belinda I grew up in the bay area and am the younger sister to Ellen and older sister to Albert on the panel. Later I went to Harvard, graduated class of 2017 studied computer science with a secondary in phycology, and now I'm at google where I am a product manager.

*Kevin Bryan:* Hey guys I'm Kevin, a rising junior at the University of Pennsylvania, and I'm majoring in neuroscience and am an editor for the Daily Pennsylvanian, the independent student newspaper. If you're interested in anything in these areas, please let me know. I am excited to be here.

*Albert Zheng:* Great so why don't we hop right into the Q&A? So, the first question for the panel is, what is the most important thing to do when preparing for college applications? Obviously, this is a very broad topic so any thoughts you have will be greatly appreciated.

*Belinda Zheng:* So, I think I'll go first. If you are thinking of the college application process, I think that just one thing to keep in mind is that this isn't just a quick one-shot thing in senior year. It is especially important for those of you that are earlier on in high school. Really, you should see the college application process as the best presentation of your own strengths and skills, and that's often easy and helpful to start earlier on. So even if the college application does not start until the senior year, it's often helpful to think about what you're good at and what you want to start developing as skills. Like what would a good application for you look like? A lot of these things take time, like building leadership skills or ending up as an officer in a certain club, or even founding your own club, if that's what you're interested in. A lot of these things take a lot of time and a lot of planning, and it's helpful to think of the whole application process in a holistic way and think about it long-term.

*Albert Zheng:* Great answer, does anyone want to add to that?

*Valerie Morales:* I could add to that. Think about if you want to do something, a particular profession, and a range of areas specializing in that profession. If you don't know what your professional goal is, I think you'd really think about the type of environment you'd want to be in and find different schools you would like to attend. I think one of the things I learned in retrospect is that there are a lot more universities out there than you really know about or your friends and family know about because the world is very big.

*Albert Zheng:* Great, thank you for those responses. Those are very helpful. Kind of going off of one of the things that were mentioned when I started to prepare for college applications earlier. The next question is when should students begin to prepare for college applications? Is there a time that is too early, or too late?

*Kevin Bryan:* I can go for this one. I think at the end of the day, it really does depend on your ability to time manage and how many activities you're juggling. I think you should always play it by ear, but I think gathering your application materials earlier is better. In my personal experience, in terms of actually preparing application materials such as essays, activity lists, etc., I think that the summer before is a really nice place to start. Start really thinking about what the activities list is going to be early on in the summer, especially because you have more time in the summer and because the earlier applications will be due later that fall. Essays require more rewrites than you think. Of course, actual activities themselves should have been started much earlier, like the beginning of high school to show a continuity of interest. (Edited by KB)

*Albert Zheng:* Great Thank you for that. Does anyone else have anything to add?

*Belinda Zheng:* Yeah, I can just add to that. I totally agree with what Kevin Bryan said. Earlier is definitely better, I would highly recommend starting over the summer before senior year for the application itself. Because I think that it can take a lot of time to figure out, to Valerie's point earlier. What colleges do you actually want to apply to? What is your overall package going to look like? And a lot of these take a lot of reflection and time to actually craft to get into a good spot. I would also say to apply earlier for schools. I think studies in data show that in general if you apply earlier there is a higher admission rate, obviously, that is more of a correlation than actual causation but I think it shows how important it is to actually plan early and start early. I would say that starting the year before is for the application itself. As I was mentioning earlier, I think you should actually start thinking about how you should craft your package, and what sort of activities you should do. What skills should you build? I would say you could even at the start of high school you can start thinking about those things. Like what sort of skills, you want to build, I always knew I was into business. I think you heard from Mr. Schmit earlier but I joined DECA (business club). That's how I met him, and that's something I started thinking about freshman year of high school. So, I would just say for the application itself to start as early as possible, probably the summer before your senior year of high school. For actually planning your package itself and what activities to do, I would say that's much earlier.

*Albert Zheng:* Ok great thank you for those responses, they were very insightful. This is going to be our last question, sorry it's a little bit short but we want to make sure we can keep going with the schedule. If you guys have follow-up questions make sure to reach out to the organizers and they could relay questions to us. The last question for this panel is, what was impactful for you personally to apply for college? For example, was it an extracurricular, was it a class, was it your SAT scores? Just talk through your own experiences about what was one thing that was very important.

*Ellen Zheng:* I can weigh in here, I think for me it was definitely the teachers and professors that I had more than anything. It felt like a good opportunity to sort of broaden my horizons and know what other possibilities were out there and become the first of my family to not become an engineer immediately and instead go to law school, for example, that was something I was interested in the longer term. So, meeting diverse types of people, especially through my teachers was super helpful for me to broaden my horizons.

*Albert Zheng:* Great, does anyone have anything to add to that?

*Luis Perez:* Yeah, I can add a little bit of color from my side, teachers definitely made a big difference both as role models, and also as people who can encourage you to look a little outside of what colleges you may be aware of at the time. Definitely, the other thing that made a difference is just kind of, and these come up with Belinda and Valerie as well, trying to be strategic about what college you are applying for. You really want to find the ones that are the right fit for the narrative that you have built up, the skill sets that you have and the person you want to be in the future. It really helps to have a support network of people that can give you insights into the many different professions you might take on later, as well as introduce you to many colleges and paths to get you eventually to the place where you want to be.

*Albert Zheng:* Great, thank you so much for your responses, guys. Sorry again for having to cut this so short, if you have more questions please talk to the organizers and they can reach out to us. Thank you, guys, so much for listening to us and I will pass it back to the emcees.

# 2022 Youth International Environment Protection Awareness Conference

## Introductions

Hello, and welcome to the 8th annual International Cultural Exchange Conference Focused on Teens! This has been the seventh annual Youth International Environment Protection Awareness Conference. The purpose is to have professionals and students exchange information and ideas about what we can do to help the environment. We have translated, transcribed, compiled, and edited the speeches of all our speakers.

## Acknowledgments

We would like to thank all of our guest speakers for attending and providing us with such insightful speeches. We also thank our hosts for keeping the conference running smoothly, as well as the technology department for making sure the PowerPoint was functioning properly. Thank you to all the students who translated on stage, as well as those who transcribed and translated speeches for our proceedings.

*Editors of Environment Conference Proceedings:*
Suri Zheng, Kevin Zhang

*English to Chinese Translators and Interpreters:*
Siqi Li, Yiming (Amelia) Wang, Bo W.

*Proceedings Transcription:*
Allen Bryan/Edward Bryan, Yiming (Amelia) Wang

*Technical Support:*
Yiming (Amelia) Wang

*Hosts:*
Siqi Li, Allen Bryan, Owen Ouyang, Yiming Wang, Kevin Zhang

# Dr. Jay Jones

**Dr. Jay Jones** has a broad academic background, with concentrations in Botany, Microbiology, Chemistry, and Geology. His research and work experience includes Senior Research Geobotanist, researching oil and gas exploration (ARCO), Naturalist/Interpreter (National Park Service), and Remote Sensing Consultant (NASA/Lockheed). He is currently in the field conducting floral surveys, as well as in the laboratory working with complex analytical instrumentation. As a Professor of Biology and Biochemistry, Jones has taught an exceptionally broad range of courses including versions of an interdisciplinary course entitled: Toward a Sustainable Planet. Many of these courses have field components in which faculty and students see the global impact of the human species in various countries around the world.

## What Should We Do to Move Toward a Sustainable Civilization?

Thank you. As Carl Schmidt said, it's a very complicated problem. It's global warming on a global scale and it's climate change in each place. So, some places may be cooling, some places may be warming.

So, let's first look at the problem. In every talk that I give, because it is so fundamental, I talk about the population. Approximately six years ago, the population of the world was approximately 7.3 billion people. And, July 15th, the population was approximately 7.8 billion people. Oh, excuse me, 7.8 billion in 2021 a year ago, and this year it's 7.9. So, we've added over 132 million people in one year.

Everybody has to eat; everybody has to have resources.

We have populated the earth like bacteria on a Petri plate. Microbiology was one of my majors, and I can tell you when a Petri plate looks like that, there is not long until the Petri plate is full. This arrow has been displaced, it should be pointing to the rising part of the curve, which is where we are now. Population growth is starting to slow, but not fast enough to give a sustainable economy.

The human ecological footprint, that is, our impact on the world around us, is a function of: population size, per capita consumption, and other factors, such as what we're consuming, the waste products that we produce, and so forth.

I'd like to introduce the concept of an overshoot day. If we look at all of the people on earth and we consider how much of the environmental resources could be allotted to everybody, that is our ecological footprint that would be our share. However, not all countries use their share. The United States is one of the countries that use far more than our share. In the United States, we used our share up by March 13th. We are now using more than our share. In China, the overshoot date was June 2nd. I recently came back from Malawi, Rwanda, and Zambia. All three of those countries do not have an overshoot date. Each individual, the individual per capita consumption, is within their allotment. If we look at the overshoot date for the whole earth, not just individual countries, we find that we started using more resources than could be sustained in 1970. And by 2021, we were using more resources as a species than the environment can support by July 29th.

We talk about carbon dioxide in the atmosphere and other greenhouse gasses but land use is a major factor in climate change as well. You change what we call the Albedo, or the reflectivity, of how bright the surface of the earth is when we do things like farm an area, mine an area, or spread garbage around.

And we have many other impacts as well, these externalities if you will. Pollution of the water, and also toxic materials that are in the air. Microplastics and so forth, are now standard in our environment everywhere on earth.

So, we have tremendously changed the surface of the earth. What you see on the left is a small patch of tall grass prairie which no longer exists over most of the United States nor in other countries as well. Instead, it is replaced by what you see in the upper right-hand corner, with managed farms, and feeding facilities for livestock, and the native species, as Carl Schmidt pointed out, have been largely excluded. What you see on the right-hand lower side is a pile of bison skeletons that were harvested for phosphate fertilizer as they were exterminated, in part to exterminate indirectly the aboriginal populations so that the land could be privatized. Again, the arrows here are displaced. These are feedlots with literally thousands of cattle, causing water pollution and air pollution. Deforestation is rampant around the world. Rainforests covered 14% of the earth's surface and it's now down to 6%. The deltas and estuaries are also being developed. They are also subsiding, which is a natural geologic process and with the rise in sea level, these highly productive zones have a very short life ahead of them. We cannot easily replace these, and that means there will be fewer resources to share among the growing population. Coastal impacts. This is how most seafood is produced – that is the mussels and the other types of seafood – they're being farmed. 80% of salmon, for instance, is actually farmed. Such intense agriculture, or aquaculture, in this case, devastates the environment. This slide blows me away. This is a hog farm. So, each of these multistoried structures will house hogs, in an enclosed environment. This has its own granary, and the amount of waste that will be produced is phenomenal, causing a devastating environmental situation. Such operations create many externalities.

Okay, major consequences of the environmental problem. As we develop the earth, and as our GDP or GNP increases, what we see is that there is less and less room for wildlife. We're losing species at a phenomenal rate. Faster than the transition of any of the three eras or five extinctions that have occurred in the past. We could eliminate 99.999%+ and we would never be on any list of concerned species or threatened species or species to watch. So, extinction is not necessarily an indication of the health of the environment.

Climate change. We've talked about that. Droughts, floods, wildfires. Hot and cold weather. The weather kills more people than floods do. Disrupted biological communities. More severe weather, rising sea level. All of these have a cost. And the question is, with the costs that we would have to bear to turn the course away from fossil fuels and better land use, etc., how do we convince people to make that investment now to avoid what's going to be a much larger bill down the road?

I don't think that there's any way that we can actually convince governments and people, the majority of people, to make those changes.

These are just some photos of the implications of the changes that we're seeing. This is an almond field, deprived of water. This was a desert scrub. Normally, we took water from other places and made it productive. When you don't have that water, it goes back to being a very dry environment.

I think we have to realize that all of these effects that we're seeing and all of the changes that would need to be made will have an effect on jobs and we have to look at these broadly so we can find a path for people that are displaced, etc. and to reduce our impact.

So, this is a picture of my raised bed in my front yard. I planted my whole backyard, so this is in my front yard, last year. This is my front yard this year, because of the limited water. This is representative of food from my garden last year on July 15th. And this is July 15th of this year. Now think about this on a global scale. It's not just my garden. So, with the loss of agricultural productivity, there's less food. That means the prices are going to go up. It's not just a function of water availability, it's a function of the soil texture, it's a function of the deposition of salts in the soil, and as a phenomenon, we're hearing disaster in terms of the cost of food and our ability to support the world's population. And the human environmental impact is not affecting everybody equally. And it will even be more unequal in the future. It simply depends on your geographic location, the wealth that you have, the resources you have available to you, and to some extent your profession, your self-sufficiency, your support network, government policies, and so forth.

There are many people in the world now that are suffering from the impact of pollution, from the impact of food scarcity, and water scarcity. So, many have already been affected. When we think of the environment, we tend to think of it as something that's going to affect us in the future. However, again, on a global scale, many have already been affected. Millions have been affected, and more are being affected every day. This just is an illustration of the inequality in living conditions. And it shows that some countries, like those that have an overshoot date early in the year, bear more responsibility for environmental deterioration than those in other countries.

Okay, so in summary, the global environment is changing at an ever-increasing rate. It's happening faster and faster, exceeding the predictions of scientists. It's largely driven by human technology and practices. Yes, there are a lot of natural factors, but when you factor those out, in statistical modeling, you see that human technology and practices are having the biggest effect right now.

The consequences of these changes cannot be accommodated with our current operating system, and I include in that our current economic system. So, we must work to change our behavior. Life is now changing dramatically and we must act.

So, what can we do and what should we do? We need to change our worldview and economic paradigm, and a change in the economic paradigm is required. We live in a consumption economy. You want to come up with a product you can sell, and make a profit. And we buy far too many things that we do for a quality life. I'm not saying that we should go back to a hunter-gatherer type of modality, we cannot do that. But the worldview of a hunter-gatherer world is really what should be guiding us. Mr. Schmidt talked about the tragedy of the commons. In aboriginal philosophies, the commons were considered as having values. Each of the elements: the plants, the animals, and even the geological components. And when you have a culture that has that kind of view, the tragedy of the commons is not so tragic. The western way of looking at things is not compatible with sustainability. The differences between the aboriginal ways of looking at things, again, don't look at the ecological resources as a commodity for us to use, necessarily. There is a unity of the world around us, that is, the plants, the animals, the geologic environment, and ourselves. So, we are a part of the system, we are not apart from the system with the rest of the world to be here for us. This is largely a function of the Abrahamic traditions. Christianity, Islam, and Jewish cultures.

In our local area, we have aboriginals that go by the name of the Tongva. Humans were viewed not as the apex of creation, but as a strand of the web of life. And their traditions reflect this. Do we look at a plate of food, and thank the plant? And if we eat a chicken, do we thank the chicken? The aboriginal ways of looking at things are displaced by the western world's ways of looking at things, with capitalism and exploitation of natural resources.

This is particularly illustrated by the loss of languages. Because languages are an element, an essential element, of each culture. And when you wipe out, or when you transform a culture, into the western way, the materialistic way of looking at things, essentially the language disappears. And we're losing languages at a very fast rate. But what that means is that we're losing cultures that have that connection to nature at a very fast rate. This is the number, the percentage of languages lost in 1920. This is the situation today. Very few cultures, very few people, have sensitivity to the environment. Very few cultures are surviving.

I just came back from Malawi and Rwanda, and in Malawi for instance, the villages that I stayed in, there were no fences. The common environment was shared by all. And this is one of the countries that have no overshoot day. People seemed to be reasonably happy but had some needs as well.

So, what are the solutions? I think the solutions have to be an individual thing because, on a grand scale, I don't think there is any hope of changing directions. But individually, we should be informed. We should simplify our life and reduce our footprint. And we have to target all areas of life. The small things add up. We should support system-wide efforts to change, but our individualism is probably more appropriate and effective. There's still room for entrepreneurs and such to develop appropriate technologies and things that are needed. Concentrate on the quality of life, not how much we own. Not much hope at this level, I don't think. We need an economic paradigm shift. What happens when you use less stuff? You put people out of work. It's complicated. You gotta be able to shift people to appropriate technologies, but the bottom line is we gotta use less stuff. Perhaps even not working as much, but rather fixing things, rather than buying new stuff. All sorts of things would have to change. If there is a place to have a quality life, it will need to be assembled at the community level. I do not see it happening at the national level. In essence, it's a matter of personal values and integrity. Uh oh, I used the term "values". What am I supposed to say? I need to look at that chart again. Personal values and integrity. We really can't blame the government and big business for everything. If we look at industrial agriculture and so forth, if we buy the product, we are essentially voting for those practices. Let me repeat that. buy the products that are causing environmental problems, we are voting for that environmental degradation. So, our dollars or our RMB.

I have to talk about palm oil. This is the last segment. I have seen the devastation caused by palm oil production. In Borneo, I have seen it also in Costa Rica, and it is occurring in other places around the world, displacing some of the most diverse biological communities on earth. In previous talks, I have discussed and shown a sample of the animals and some of the plants that are being displaced and farmed to extinction. This is a palm oil truck out the bus window. And palm oil is in just about all of the products you're going to find, believe it or not. You'd find it in just about everything these days. Nutella is largely palm oil. So, when I say we vote with our dollars or our RMB, when we buy these products, we are in essence endorsing deforestation. A couple of years ago, I was hosted, my students and I were hosted by the Malaysian palm oil board, and so they're not bad people, it's just that the implications, those externalities of what they're promoting, are not consistent with sustainability.

This is one of the little critters in the field station that is threatened because this animal cannot live in an oil palm plantation. Next slide. Well, this is my grandson. I'm an old guy, I lived during a good time in the history of humanity, but I worry about the future for you, young folk, and this little guy as well.

Yeah, so any questions, thoughts, or comments, we'll probably handle those at the end of the thing in our discussion. But if you take down my email address, I'll be glad to share information that I've collected throughout the years in my various roles. We're all in this together. Thank you.

# Carl Schmidt

**Carl Schmidt** is a Business Education teacher at Monte Vista High School in Cupertino, California. He is one of the founders of Silicon Valley DECA, one of three California Districts. He just ended his second term as Chairperson of the California Association of DECA.

Mr. Schmidt completed his undergraduate work in Economics and later earned both a Masters of Business Administration (International Business) and a Master of Arts in Education (Educational Leadership). Prior to his teaching career, he was a senior consultant for Price Waterhouse in New York City and both a Manager, Information Systems and Materials Manager for Xerox Corporation's Southern California Manufacturing Operations. He also had the opportunity to serve as a co-founder and Executive Vice President of a Global Electronics start-up.

## Environmental Issues

The first thing I want to say is, if we had solutions to the problems and we all agreed upon that, we would've solved them. So, solutions are not an easy matter. First of all, we have the origin point of view. Second, we all have the consensus of what we want to do, and third, we have to determine who's gonna bear the cost and who's gonna bear the burden of any solution. So, this evening we are gonna talk about some concepts here: the tragedy of the commons, market solutions, industrialization & externalities, trade-offs in public policy, global warming, climate change, and the Green New Deal.

Let's talk about the tragedy of the commons. Now, this is a basic concept that says if we do not have private property—now I understand many people don't accept the cost of private property. Some people believe property is staffed, but in the western world, one of the pillars of capitalism is private property. Well, you don't have that, you have a common area, and you have a whole community that is eligible to use that common area. What happens, it's gonna be overused and is gonna be depleted, because there is no incentive for anyone to reduce his/her consumption. Now when we think about the tragedy of the commons, the ocean is one of our commons, no one owns it, and we all own it in common. The air that we breathe, no one owns that, we own that in common, and it's like a city park, none owns it, the city owns it and nobody takes responsibility and it becomes dirty, filthy, and it's a crime. So again, the concept here is people continue adding cows to the common area for grazing until such a point it's overpopulated and depleted of its nutrients. So, the incentive is to get what you can get while you can get it and before it's gone. Now if the next slide will show us an example of what are some of the commonalities we encounter. Greenhouse gasses, overgrazing, non-renewable resources, population growth deforestation, and overfishing. We talk about California being short of water. We talk about Arizona being short of water and Nevada. Most of those states are deserts and we are officially provided water for them to use. But what happens is by providing that water cheap we have more people moving and an even greater demand for that particular water. I can't envision a country like the United States having people move from those areas, so we are going to find ways at this particular point to provide water to users of agriculture and populations, and that in turn will draw more business to California and the demands of water will be even greater. So, in recognizing this condition in economics, this is a condition of scarcity. So, there are very few goods that we can use that cost us nothing. Private property, a pillar of capitalism, is one of the things that we have to deal with. The challenge we have in market economics is there are third parties who are not a part of the transactions who are paying a cost.

Let's go back to the issue of the growth of the US. When we start to go westward from the 13 colonies, there are no incentives for people to take care of the land. Today people go from east to west and southwest, where water is scarce. And there are many unintended consequences like scarcity of water/drought, energy consumption, depletion of wildlife habitat, extinction/ near-extinction of plant and animal species, expensive land, and overcrowding.

Industrialization and post-Industrialization are both driven by cost, efficiency & technology. The goal of corporations today is to produce where it is least costly and to sell at the best price and return on investment. All the new energy forms we are using today—wind, water, electricity, and coal—all produce pollutants. And energy sources like coal mines are also important, they produce a lot of jobs. If they are gone, many people will lose their jobs. Nuclear power, though, is 24/7 but people won't take the risk of living around it. Wind turbines also have a lot of problems such as killing birds. Our situation is becoming more complicated.

There is a long debate about whether the situation should be called global warming or climate change. Scientists attribute the global warming trend observed since the mid-20th century to human contributions to the "greenhouse effect"—warming those results when the atmosphere traps heat radiating from Earth toward space. Certain gasses in the atmosphere block heat from escaping. Long-lived gasses that remain semi-permanently in the atmosphere and do not respond physically or chemically to changes in temperature are described as "forcing" climate change. Gasses, such as water vapor, which respond physically or chemically to changes in temperature are seen as "feedbacks." The atmosphere of Venus, like Mars, is nearly all carbon dioxide. But Venus has about 154,000 times as much carbon dioxide in its atmosphere as Earth (and about 19,000 times as much as Mars does), producing a runaway greenhouse effect and a surface temperature hot enough to melt lead. On Earth, human activities are changing the natural greenhouse. Over the last century, the burning of fossil fuels like coal and oil has increased the concentration of atmospheric carbon dioxide ($CO_2$). This happens because the coal or oil burning process combines carbon with oxygen in the air to make $CO_2$. To a lesser extent, the clearing of land for agriculture, industry, and other human activities has increased concentrations of greenhouse gasses. It's reasonable to assume that changes in the Sun's energy output would cause the climate to change since the Sun is the fundamental source of energy that drives our climate system. Indeed, studies show that solar variability has played a role in past climate changes. For example, a decrease in solar activity coupled with an increase in volcanic activity is thought to have helped trigger the Little Ice Age between approximately 1650 and 1850, when Greenland cooled from 1410 to the 1720s and glaciers advanced in the Alps. In its Fifth Assessment Report, the Intergovernmental Panel on Climate Change, a group of 1,300 independent scientific experts from countries all over the world under the auspices of the United Nations, concluded there's a more than 95 percent probability that human activities over the past 50 years have warmed our planet. In the foreseeing future, we are going to manufacture in those areas which have fewer restrictions regarding the environment.

Thank you very much for your time, and hopefully, we will have a discussion later.

# Kevin Zhang

<hr>

**Kevin Zhang** is a rising 12th grader who attends Mountain View High School in Mountain View, California. He enjoys computer science, physics, math, and history.

## The Role of Nuclear Power

Hello everyone, I'll be talking about the role of nuclear power in today's world. So first off, how do nuclear reactors work? Nuclear reactors use nuclear fission - the process of splitting atoms - to produce energy as heat. Inside a reactor, this heat creates steam which spins a turbine to produce electricity. Reactors use radioactive materials such as uranium as fuel. Water is also used as a coolant and a neutron moderator, or a material used to slow down the speed of neutrons to maintain a fission reaction.

What is the current role that nuclear energy has in energy production? Currently, 439 nuclear reactors are operating worldwide, with 94 in the US and 52 in China. The average nuclear reactor produces around 1 GW of energy annually. Nuclear power currently accounts for around 10% of the world's electricity, 20% of power in the US, and 5% of energy in China. Nuclear also accounts for ⅓ of all low-carbon electricity worldwide and is second after hydropower.

Of course, there are no perfect sources of energy, and I will now be talking about the major pros and cons of using nuclear energy. Nuclear energy is completely carbon-free, which means it is a large step towards reducing carbon emissions on earth. It also uses significantly less land than other types of renewable energy. It has a high energy output and is a highly reliable source of energy (plants in the United States were running at full efficiency 92% of the time in 2021). On the other side, uranium, the main fuel for nuclear reactors, is non-renewable and costs will only increase. Prices to construct nuclear reactors are also very expensive, and maintenance and repair costs continue to be high. Reactors also produce nuclear waste that is harmful to the environment. And while very rare, malfunctions of reactors can be catastrophic, as we have seen.

What issues is the ongoing debate on nuclear energy focused around? Energy security issues correlate in a large part with increasing support for nuclear energy. Nuclear energy provides many countries with energy independence. For example, the 1973 oil embargo by OPEC caused countries to look further toward investing in nuclear energy after fossil fuel prices increased sharply. Additionally, increased attention to the climate change movement and concerns about a global energy shortage has renewed interest in nuclear energy. Sustainability is another issue concerning nuclear energy. Long-term management of nuclear waste produced by reactors remains an issue. A significant hindrance to the further proliferation of nuclear energy is public fear of nuclear accidents, a fear which has been largely ingrained by incidents in the past. Nuclear energy fuels such as uranium and plutonium can also be reprocessed for the creation of nuclear weapons, which remains an international concern.

How is nuclear energy projected to grow in the future? In recent years, there has been a decrease in electricity growth demand, and financing for many nuclear plants around the world has become scarcer. A dozen plants have closed in the US in the last decade due to rising competition from cheap sources of natural gas and increasing maintenance and repair costs for reactors. However, nuclear energy worldwide is expected to grow by 20% by 2030 and 80% by 2050. China currently has an ambitious vision for nuclear energy, with plans to expand domestic nuclear energy production from 55 gigawatts annually in 2021 to between 120 and 150 gigawatts annually by 2030. China also plans to build 30 overseas reactors in its Belt and Road Initiative. ITER, or the International Thermonuclear Experimental Reactor, is an international project to develop a nuclear reactor using fusion - the process of joining two nuclei into one to produce energy - and has been in progress since 2007.

That's it, thanks for listening.

# Allen Bryan

**Allen Bryan** is an 11th-grade student at Junipero Serra High school in California. He is interested in the STEM and pre-med fields. He is starting his own Pre-med club to help students at his school gain knowledge and interest in science, as well as finding opportunities for them, such as internships. He also expresses his love for music through his school Jazz Band and classical music playing. He also plays football and runs track for his school.

## Coliforms Indicate Contamination of Waterways

Our waterways are critical resources for wildlife and human activity. Increasing levels of human encroachment and overpopulation have caused waterways to become more contaminated. Waterways are popular for recreational activities including kayaking, windsurfing, rowing, swimming, and fishing in America. I enjoy kayaking along San Francisco Bay. More importantly, in some parts of the world, waterways are an essential source of drinking water.

Bacterial contamination of the earth's waterways can have devastating consequences. For example, according to the World Health Organization (WHO), cholera from contaminated water kills up to 143,000 people per year. The Gates Foundation provides even more dramatic numbers that show "1200 hundred children under the age of 5" die every day due to waterborne diseases. The ultimate solution is to clean our waterways and provide adequate water and sewer systems for all people on earth. Until that time, we have to monitor the safety of the water. One way is to use indicator species.

Testing water for all pathogens is impractical and costly. Many pathogens can only be grown under very rigorous conditions. More advanced methods, like polymerase chain reaction (PCR), may show the presence of pathogens, but do a poor job of quantifying their number. The main source of disease from water is fecal contamination. Therefore, tests have been developed to look for indicator fecal bacteria. Coliform bacteria are found in the intestines of mammals and birds and therefore increased levels of these bacteria may suggest higher levels of fecal bacteria in the environment. These high levels indicate that water may be polluted with bacterial species that cause cholera, typhoid fever, and gastroenteritis. One type of intestinal bacteria, *Escherichia coli* (*E. coli*), is a coliform species that is always assumed to indicate the presence of fecal contamination. The United States Environmental Protection Agency (EPA) recommends a cutoff for water safety of 410 colony forming units (cfu) of *E. coli* per 100 ml.

To better understand the extent and causes of bacterial contamination of waterways near our home on the San Francisco Bay, we studied Redwood City, CA waterways. We used an optimized form of a standard colorimetric assay (Coliscan Easygel ®, Micrology labs) to differentiate coliforms and *E. coli* from other naturally occurring bacteria. Samples from four different waterways feeding into the bay were collected on two different dates, for a total of 8 tests. Pink colonies showed us general coliform bacteria, while blue bacterial colonies showed a specific coliform species, *E. coli.*

We found higher levels of coliforms and *E. coli* in waterways after heavy 9-day rain when compared to samples taken before the rain. At one location, the Belmont Slough, coliforms, and *E. coli* levels far exceeded the EPA standard, with almost double the 410 colonies forming unit (cfu) cutoff. This indicated that at least one waterway feeding into the San Francisco Bay was unsafe for human activity. While it is likely that each rain washes pet and wildlife fecal material into waterways, the high cfu count after nine straight days of rain may suggest another cause. In at least one other area of the bay, the rain had caused an overflow of local sewage systems. To our knowledge, no overflow had been reported for the Belmont Slough. This means that our part of the bay was unsafe and no one knew about it.

What can we do to protect populations from unsafe waterways? There are many causes of bacterial contamination of waterways around the world, but human waste is the primary source of danger because human waste is more likely to carry human disease. We can help control and avoid illness resulting from contamination by tracking and monitoring the levels of coliforms in waterways at all times (Especially after heavy rains). We can also increase monitoring of sewage systems near bodies of water to make sure leakages and overflow will never occur. When results show that waterways are dangerous to the public, warnings should be posted to alert every one of the current danger. If contaminated water is the only source of drinking water, educate the population on how to properly treat water to reduce the likelihood of illness. For example, bringing water to a rolling boil for three minutes before consuming it can kill most pathogens. For your safety, before using a natural waterway, always look for signs posted to indicate contamination of water.

Finally, more worldwide funding of sewage and water systems is key. The Gates Foundation is one organization that is heavily invested in solutions for water treatment and alternative sewage treatment methods. These man-made alternatives can take pressure off of nature, providing cleaner, healthier waterways.

# Kevin Gong

**Kevin Gong** is a rising junior at W.T. Woodson High School, a public school in Fairfax Virginia. He enjoys learning world history and biology during school. During his free time, he likes to listen to music.

## Mountain Fires and Their Impact

Mountain fires have many names such as wildfires, forest fires, and forest blazes, which are a type of fire that usually occurs in the forest and wilderness that is difficult to control. Usually caused by lightning, some other common causes are human negligence such as smoking, camping, using a lighter in the forest, intentional arson, volcanic eruptions, volcanic ash clouds, heat waves, droughts, and cyclical climate shifts. These can all significantly increase the risk of mountain fire.

Greenpeace declared in 2018 that "global wildfire emissions a total amount of 7.7 billion metric tons of $CO_2$ per year. You may think that this is a huge number of fountain fires, but if you look back to 2020 there was a huge mountain fire that happened in Australia. Mountain fires happen constantly all over the world, so this number has become normal.

When wildfires occur, ash and chemicals can flow into waterways, making drinking water sources unsafe. Wildfires can damage water treatment facilities, causing drinking water unsafe. However, even if water sources and treatment facilities are not damaged, drinking water in buildings and buried water distribution systems can be chemically contaminated. This is because the soil around the distribution system is heated up by the mountain fires, which causes chemical effects inside the tube of the distribution system.

After the wildfire, the danger remains. Residents returning to their homes may be at risk from falling burned trees. Living creatures may fall into ash pits.

The risk after other fires may increase if other weather extremes occur. For example, wildfires reduce the ability of the soil to absorb precipitation, so heavy rainfall could lead to more severe damage such as flooding and mudslides.

Aerial fire extinguishing is a way of using an airplane or helicopter to extinguish a fire from the air. This can be done more effectively while reducing the number of casualties.

Artificial rainfall is achieved by lowering the temperature in the clouds and causing the water vapor in the clouds to condense.

Prevention techniques are designed to manage air quality, maintain ecological balance, protect resources, and influence future fires.

Ways to prevent Mountain Fires:

1. Try not to use fire sources in the forest.

2. Artificial rainfall in dry forest areas.

3. Use tools such as chainsaws in the forest to put out sparks as soon as they arise.

4. Employ more forest rangers so that forest fires can be detected earlier.

5. Supply planes to the fire department. For forest fires, planes will be very effective in extinguishing fires.

6. Increase the manpower of the fire department.

# Suri Zheng

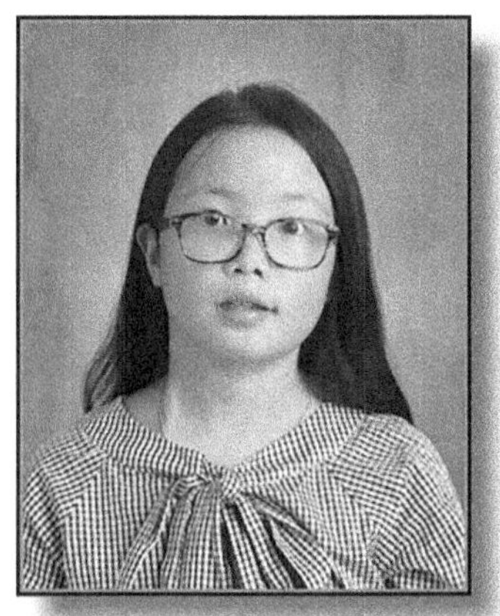

**Suri Zheng** is an incoming sophomore at Palo Alto High School (Paly). Her hobbies include doing arts and crafts, hanging out with her friends, and playing the piano.

## The Dangers of Cattle

Are cattle good? Well, they provide nutrients for the body to keep you healthy but sometimes even cattle can be harmful.

### *How Do Cattle Release Methane?*

Cattle have methane stored in their guts and 89% of that is released into the atmosphere through their nose or mouth when they eat. That is a lot, considering that one cattle can produce 220 pounds of methane in only a year.

### *Why is Methane bad for the Environment?*

Methane is bad for the environment because it is a potent factor in causing greenhouse gas emissions. Just cattle alone can produce 14.5% of the global greenhouse gasses. Although methane is shorter-lived than carbon dioxide, it is still 28 times more harmful than $CO_2$.

### *What can we do to help?*

One thing we can help with is by reducing the amount of beef we eat. If we cut down our intake of beef by 50%, either by eating beef less regularly or reducing the amount eaten each day then that would reduce the amount of demand for meat, thus, reducing the population of cattle by 50%. That can reduce our carbon emissions by 43 gigatons yearly!

### *Why is eating a lot of beef terrible for our health?*

Beef can be good and provide nutrients and protein for your body; but if you overeat beef, it can cause heart disease, shorten your lifespan, cause types of cancers and kidney problems and make you have digestive issues.

Considering the dangers above, next time you eat beef you can consider switching to a better option that will help keep you and our planet healthier.

Thank you.

# Winford Chang

**Winford Chang** is a 15-year-old student in Las Vegas, Nevada. Currently, he is attending A-Tech High School as a computer science major. He has many hobbies which include cooking, football, martial arts, and guitar. In his free time, he loves to hang out with friends and work out.

## Global Warming, the Ozone Layer, and Greenhouse Gasses

Around the world, greenhouses are used to help grow and nurture plants. Greenhouses take the outside light and convert it into heat and trap it inside to keep plants warm and protected from the outside. Because of all the excess heat involved in a greenhouse, their rooms are kept warm from day to night and even keep the plants warmed up and safe during the winter. What if, though, I told you that our planet itself is just like a Greenhouse? This is called the greenhouse effect.

Built-up gasses called the atmosphere help keep the earth warm and the sun's deadly rays out. The earth, though, still needs to release some heat and it's starting to keep more and more unnecessary heat, this is because the greenhouse gasses, some examples being nitrous oxide, carbon dioxide, water vapor, and methane, are all needed to be kept in balance and more of them means that they trap more heat. Burning fossil fuels such as coal and oil releases more and more carbon dioxide into the atmosphere. Greenhouse gasses are being observed by NASA as they grow more and more abundant in the atmosphere. As they are released, having all of this information allows us to slow down the buildup of greenhouse gasses and maybe even, hopefully, slowly reverse the damage that we have already done to it.

Even though it is getting hotter and hotter we should still be grateful for the greenhouse effect. The four greenhouse gasses help keep out the sun's worst radiation and let through invisible light so we can see. They are located around 6 kilometers off the earth's crust and catch the infrared waves and vibrate strongly before sending out a different infrared light in a different direction. Without the greenhouse gasses to keep us warm and insulated from the sun the average temperature would be -18° Celsius daily.

# Siqi Li

**Siqi Li** is a senior at Gulliver Preparatory in Florida. Her hobbies are art and reading, she is also interested in art, sociology, and psychology.

## Plastic Pollution and Eco Brick Making

One of the most important and pressing environmental issues right now is plastic pollution. Post-World War II, the production and development of plastic products accelerated. Plastic quickly revolutionized our life. From its place in medicine to devices that provide clean water, we wouldn't be where we are today without plastic. However, this rapid development led to plastic reliance and the throw-away culture surrounding plastic use. "Today, single-use plastics account for 40 percent of the plastic produced every year" (Parker). Think about all the wrappers and plastic bags we toss away—they may have a lifespan of mere minutes but will stay in our environment for hundreds of years.

Our plastic production has been exponentially increasing, in fact, half of all plastic ever produced was produced in the last 15 years. "Every year, about 8 million tons of plastic waste escapes into the oceans from coastal nations. That's the equivalent of setting five garbage bags full of trash on every foot of coastline around the world" (Parker). These plastics can be caught up by the currents and carried around the world. Once in the elements, these plastics are broken down into microplastics, then plastic microfibers. These pollute our water, including drinking water systems, and air.

Plastic pollution has a direct effect on wildlife. Every year, millions of animals, from birds to fish to other marine organisms, are killed by plastic. Plastic is known to affect nearly 700 species, including endangered species. Nearly every species of seabird eats plastics. Thousands of seabirds and sea turtles, seals, and other marine mammals are killed each year after ingesting plastic or getting entangled in it.

So, what can we do about this crisis?

One way is to demand the largest producers of single-use plastics take responsibility and find better alternatives. For example, by adding plastic additives degradant concentrates, or PDCs, to make biodegradable plastics. Other options include paper, bamboo, glass, etc. We can also be more conscious when purchasing, choosing biodegradable and or reusable products over single-use plastic and choosing more ethical brands.

It is also important to support legislation and or politicians that care about the environment and support curbing plastic production and waste.

An at-home solution to curb personal plastic waste is making ecobricks. The method was originally developed in the Philippines as a solution to two problems: a shortage of shelter; and a build of poor quality, non-recyclable plastic waste dumped on them by the West. An ecobrick usually is a plastic bottle that is densely packed with clean pieces of plastic that act as a construction block. It contains used plastics, preventing them from degrading into toxins and microplastics. Ecobricking is both an individual and collective effort, and by promoting the personal eco-bricking process, it has been claimed that it raises environmental awareness. Making an eco-brick is not a simple process, it can be quite laborious. It demands the maker to interact with the plastic waste they produce, thus creating an ecological consciousness, leading to a steady decrease in the maker's consumption of non-reusable plastic, as the Global Ecobrick Alliance claims. This movement emerged from a growing awareness of the scale of plastic pollution, the effects of said plastic pollution, and the inability of industrial recycling facilities to properly handle plastic waste.

To make an eco-brick, you would need a clean, transparent, polyethylene terephthalate (PET) plastic bottle. The plastic is cut or ripped into smaller pieces and then manually packed with a stick. To ensure that the plastic is evenly compacted throughout the bottle, rotate the bottle along the way. It is important to make sure that both the bottle and the plastic are clean and dry to avoid bacteria growth. The denser the completed ecobrick is, the better–this allows it to bear the weight of a person without deforming, minimize flammability, and increase durability/reusability.

So, what can eco bricks do? As said before, ecobricks act as a construction block, thus, it's able to build furniture, gardens, play parks, structures, and more. However, it is a big responsibility to build with ecobricks, as they need to be clean, dense, and secure.

Overall, eco-bricking may be another at-home activity that curbs plastic pollution, however, at the end of the day, simply decreasing the purchase/use of non-reusable plastics may be the best way to go in the first place. And unless our government and big corporations take action, we will always struggle with this plastic crisis.

Works Cited

Global Ecobrick Alliance. "Why Make Ecobricks?" *Ecobricks.Org*,

https://www.ecobricks.org/why/. Accessed 29 July 2022.

Parker, Laura. "Plastic Pollution Facts and Information." *National Geographic*, 7 June

2019, https://www.nationalgeographic.com/environment/article/plastic-pollution

# Matthew Li

**Matthew Li** is an incoming sophomore at Gulliver Prep. He likes to play chess and games.

## Invasive Species

### *What causes the invasion of invasive species?*

For example, wild boars consume large amounts of vegetation, destroy plants, and in some areas, may eat or uproot protected sensitive, unique, or rare plants. Often, the damaged land then becomes vulnerable to erosion. Wild Boar was deemed one of the most destructive, formidable invasive species in the United States. causing millions of dollars in agricultural damage each year, rooting and trampling through a wide variety of crops. They prey on everything from rodents and deer to endangered loggerhead sea turtles, threatening to reduce the diversity of native species. They disrupt habitats.

Invasive Species | National Wildlife Federation

### *Human activity*

Unintentionally, people often carry uninvited species with them when traveling. Ships can carry aquatic organisms in their ballast water, while smaller boats may carry them on their propellers. Insects can get into the wood of shipping pallets and crates that are shipped around the world. Some ornamental plants can escape into the wild and become invasive through the accidental spread of their seeds.

And some invasive species are intentionally or accidentally released as pets. For example, Burmese pythons are becoming a big problem in the Everglades.

How The Massive Burmese Python Has Devasted The Everglades.

Length: 16-23 Feet

Weight: Up to 200 Pounds

They have caused the Everglades' raccoon, opossum, and bobcat populations to drop by 99.3, 98.9, and 87.5 percent respectively.

The goldfish you presumed dead was flushed in the toilet:

In the Wild, Goldfish Turn From Pet to Pest - The New York Times

Goldfish swim along the bottom of lakes and rivers, uprooting vegetation, disturbing sediment, and releasing nutrients that trigger excess algal growth. They feed broadly, eating algae, small invertebrates, and fish eggs.

Lastly,

Invasive Species | National Geographic Society

Many invasive species are introduced into a new region accidentally. Zebra Mussels are native to the Black Sea and the Caspian Sea in Central Asia. Zebra Mussels arrived in the Great Lakes of North America accidentally, stuck to large ships that traveled between the two regions. There are now so many zebra mussels in the Great Lakes that they have threatened native species.

Species Introduced Intentionally

These species are introduced as a form of pest control or decorative displays.

Introduced species multiply too quickly and become invasive. For example, in 1949, five cats were brought to Marion Island, a part of South Africa in the southern Indian Ocean. The cats were introduced as pest control for mice. By 1977, about 3,400 cats were living on the island, endangering the local bird population.

Mapping the global state of invasive alien species: patterns of invasion and policy responses - Turbelin - 2017

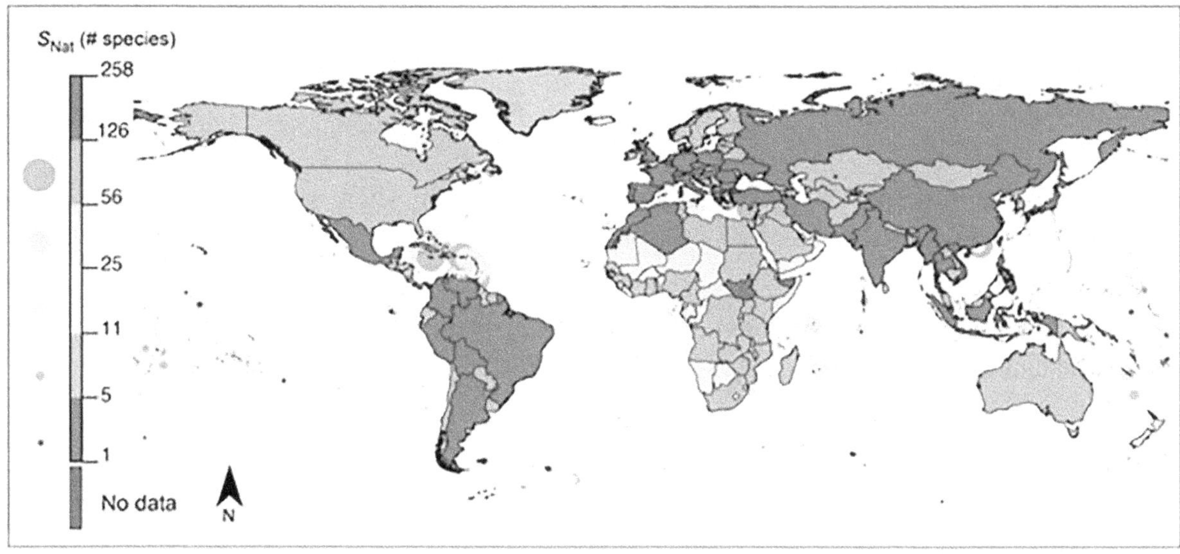


America and China

These Countries Are Most Vulnerable to Invasive Species

According to Time, Researchers also found that the United States and China act as the top sources of invasive species due to the high level of trade connected to both countries as well as the high number of invasive species already found there.

South Africa

ALIEN

In South Africa, these plants have no natural enemies such as insects, animals, and diseases that would have controlled them in their own countries.

Australia

Inside Australia's War on Invasive Species - Scientific American

Most of its wildlife is endemic, and its top predators are long extinct. This affords alien species a greater opportunity to thrive.

### Invasive plants

Many invasive plant species produce large quantities of seeds.

A plant that is both non-native and able to establish itself on many sites, grows quickly and spreads to the point of disrupting plant communities or ecosystems.

Invasive plant seeds are often distributed by birds, wind, or unknowingly humans allowing seeds to move great distances.

Some plant species produce chemicals in their leaves or root systems that inhibit the growth of other plants around them.

Invasive species have contributed to the decline of 42% of U.S. endangered and threatened species, and for 18% of U.S. endangered or threatened species, invasives are the main cause of their decline. Invasive species compete directly with native species for moisture, sunlight, nutrients, and space, decreasing overall plant diversity.

The establishment and spread of invasive species can degrade wildlife habitat, and can also result in poor-quality agricultural lands, degraded water quality, and increased soil erosion.

### Types of invasive plants

Escape of the invasives: Top six invasive plant species in the United States | Smithsonian Institution

1. Purple Loosestrife (Lythrum salicaria)

Origin: Europe and temperate Asia

Arrival: Purple loosestrife was introduced to the United States in the early 1800s for ornamental and medicinal uses.

Impact: Now growing invasively in most states, purple loosestrife can become the dominant plant species in wetlands. One plant can produce as many as 2 million wind-dispersed seeds per year and underground stems grow at a rate of 1 foot per year.

Native Alternatives: Blazing star (Liatris spicata), American blue vervain (Verbena hastate), and New York ironweed (Vernonia noveboracensis).

2. Japanese Honeysuckle (Lonicera japonica)

Origin: Eastern Asia

Arrival: One of many invasive varieties of honeysuckle in the United States, Japanese honeysuckle was brought to Long Island, NY, in 1806 for ornamental use and erosion control.C

Impact: The plant has become prolific throughout much of the East Coast as it adapts to a wide range of conditions. Japanese honeysuckle is an aggressive vine that smothers, shades, and girdles other competing vegetation. Many things eat the fruit of this plant, thereby spreading the honeysuckle's seeds

Native Alternatives: Trumpet creeper (Campsis radicans) and coral honeysuckle (Lonicera sempervirens)

3. English Ivy (Hedera helix)

Origin: Europe

Arrival: The introduction of English ivy dates back to the early 1700s when European colonists imported the plant as an easy-to-grow evergreen groundcover.

Impact: The planting and sale of English ivy continues in the United States even though it is one of the worst-spread invasive plants in the country due to its ability to handle a wide variety of conditions, particularly on the east and west coasts. English ivy is an aggressive-spreading vine that can slowly kill trees by restricting light. It spreads by vegetative reproduction and by seeds, which are consumed and spread by birds.

Native Alternatives: Creeping mint (Meehania cordata), Allegheny spurge (Pachysandra procumbens), and creeping phlox (Phlox stolonifera)

4. Kudzu (Pueraria Montana var. lobata)

Origin: China, Japan, and the Pacific islands

Arrival: Japan introduced Kudzu to the U.S. at the Philadelphia Centennial Exposition in 1876. It was first promoted as an ornamental plant and later as a forage crop in the Southeast. One million acres of

Kudzu were planted in the 1930s and 1940s by the Soil Conservation Service to reduce soil erosion on deforested lands. It was not until the 1950s that it was recognized as invasive.

Impact: Once established, Kudzu grows at a rate of up to one foot a day and 60 feet annually. This vigorous vine takes over areas in the Southeast by smothering plants and killing trees by adding immense weight and girdling or toppling them.

Native Alternatives: Carolina jessamine (Gelsemium sempervirens) and Virginia creeper (Parthenocissus quinquefolia)

5. Water hyacinth is a plant native to South America that has become an invasive species in many parts of the world. People often introduce the plant, which grows in the water, because of its pretty flowers. But the plant spreads quickly, often choking out native wildlife.

***Invasive animals:***

A non-native species that causes harm to the environment, economy, human, animal, or plant health.

<u>Invasive Species Spotlight: Armored Catfish</u>

The armored catfish (Pterygoplichthys sp.)

Originates from Central and South America. It is believed that they entered the United States around the 1950s through the aquarium trade.

Armored catfish burrow into shoreline areas, this can severely destabilize the bank, which can cause erosion. They range in size from 3 inches to over three feet in adequate conditions.

Small Indian mongoose (Herpestes auropunctatus)

Origin: Southeast Asia

Ten of the World's Most Invasive Species | Earth Rangers: Where kids go to save animals!

Impact of the introduced small Indian mongoose (Herpestes auropunctatus) on abundance and activity time of the introduced ship rat (Rattus rattus) and the small mammal community on Adriatic islands, Croatia

Introduced To Asia, Central America, and South America

Small Indian mongooses were brought over for pest control for rats and snakes.

They are aggressive predators and are blamed for the decline of the bar-winged rail (extinct), Jamaica petrel (critically endangered and possibly extinct), hawksbill turtles (critically endangered), pink pigeon (endangered), Amami rabbit (endangered), and many other birds, reptiles and mammals. Mongooses also can carry rabies and other diseases that pose a danger to humans.

***How to prevent invasive species***

Control Mechanisms | National Invasive Species Information Center).

Check equipment for accidentally carried seeds when traveling.

Check imported materials for invasive insects, seeds, and larvae.

Sanitize vehicles to get rid of insects on the vehicle.

Biological control: manipulation of natural enemies by humans (control pests by reducing the population using predators targeting invasive species)

Chemical control: the use of pesticides, herbicides, fungicides, and insecticides.

Cultural control: manipulation of habits to increase mortality of invasives or reduce their rate of damage (selection of pest-resistant crops, winter cover crops, changing planting dates).

# Yiming (Amelia) Wang

**Yiming (Amelia) Wang** is a fourth-year undergraduate student studying at Texas A&M University. She is pursuing a B.S. in Psychology and has a minor in Sociology. Meanwhile, she is also working towards graduate school for a Master's Degree in Industrial-Organizational Psychology. Her future goal is to bring a positive influence on multicultural communities and families. In her free time, Yiming enjoys dancing, cooking, reading, and spending warm afternoons with friends all around.

## Coral Bleaching

Coral reefs are large underwater structures composed of coral skeletons. Each one is a unique ecosystem with diverse collections of species that interact with each other and the physical environment. They grow slowly. Most of the substantial coral reefs found today are between 5,000 and 10,000 years old. They are most often found in warm, clear, shallow water where there's plenty of sunlight, to nurture the algae that the coral relies on for food.

Why are they important? Coral reefs are among the most biologically diverse and valuable ecosystems on Earth. An estimated 25 percent of all marine life, including over 4,000 species of fish, is dependent on coral reefs at some point in their life cycle. An estimated 1 billion people worldwide benefit from the many ecosystem services coral reefs provide including food, coastal protection, and income from tourism and fisheries. They are also valuable targets for medical research.

**Coral bleaching** is a current global crisis. When corals are stressed by changes in conditions such as water temperature, they expel the symbiotic algae living in their tissues, causing them to turn completely white.  The algae provide the coral with food and energy from the sun through photosynthesis, allowing corals to grow and reproduce. Unfortunately, without algae, most bleached corals will slowly starve to death.

So, what is the cause behind this crisis and how can we help resolve it? Since coral reefs are extremely sensitive to changes in water temperature, recent Record-breaking marine heat waves are causing mass coral bleaching globally. Climate change is the biggest threat to the Coral Reefs and is making marine heatwaves hotter, longer, and more frequent. If humans can reduce the amount of carbon pollution in the air, then it will help the seawater temperature to cool down, and that can alleviate the issue of coral bleaching.

I hope this presentation can help to raise our awareness of environmental protection. Thank you so much for listening!

# US College Panel: The Top Environmental Challenges of Today

*Albert Zeng, Harvard College Graduate (MC)*

*Ellen Zeng, Harvard Law School Graduate*

*Kevin Bryan, University of Pennsylvania*

*Luis Perez, Stanford Graduate*

*Belinda Zeng, Harvard College Graduate*

*Valerie Morales, UC Irvine*

*Kevin Bryan:* Um so yeah so that is something that many nonprofits are currently trying to address and that there is a lot of good work going in this so if you want to support charities that do that kind of work there are many out there that you can look into.

*Albert Zeng:* Thank you, that's a very great answer, is there anything anyone else wants to add?

*Ellen Zeng:* Alright, yeah, I can add something. I feel like climate change is something we are all seeing; I live in North Carolina right now and it's one of the hottest summers of all time I think the last time I read something about carbon dioxide being this high was four million years ago and these increasing global temperatures are causing a lot of problems, I think there was flooding in California recently, Kentucky, weird weather patterns everywhere, I'm excited that the U.S. Senate today I think passed a climate change bill which is pretty cool which I think should cut U.S. emissions by 40% which is like amazing progress given how much gridlock there has been.

*Albert Zeng:* Great, yeah, thank you. Cool, why don't we move on to the next question.? That is, I guess we kind of went over some of this a little bit, but what are some of the important reasons that we need to protect the environment, and what are some of the negative impacts we see if we continue to not act? I can lead off with that. Uh, I think that I live in California, and uh we've had wildfires every year or something like that, and if not every year definitely with increasing intensity in recent years. At least part of that has to do with climate change and increasing temperatures and um so that is something that is very personally affecting me or sorry I haven't been in the direct path of it recently, but you know minimum just more smog every year and yeah, I think all around the world these types of things are happening, Ella mentioned that there were flooding and conservation efforts are being affected by the increasing temperature so um that is definitely one thing.

*Belinda Zeng:* Okay, so yeah going back to the panel questions so far, one is like what are some of the important challenges we are facing concerning the environment today, and, what are some of those challenges so to speak? To add to what Albert said I would say there is also definitely an impact on species extinction. Also tying back to the first question I'm also very interested in different energy sources so I think with our current energy sources there are a lot of greenhouse gasses. There is a lot of air pollution and a lot of these can cause effects that we have already talked about with respect to climate change. Also with what Albert said you know some of these natural disasters like wildfires and I got an article from my newsfeed earlier that I found super interesting but also kind of sad about grizzly bears and how they are mating more with polar bears because polar bears are going extinct so they are kind of being forced down south and grizzly bears are going north so I think is also actually causing a lot of changes with the respect of biodiversity which I find interesting in so I think the interesting part of this conference is getting together and figuring out where we can innovate and I think through tough some of these challenges and coming up with new ideas.

*Albert Zeng:* Yeah, yeah that's true. Yeah, thank you so much for those responses and let's move on to the next question. This third question would be the last one we have planned then we can open it up to the audience; if anyone has any questions for us, we'll be happy to take them. But the last question that we had planned is what can we do as individuals to help the environment given it's such a big problem, what can we contribute?

*Kevin Bryan:* Uh yeah so uh I think one important thing is to follow government ordinances and I think one good example is right now in Salt Lake City the Salt Lake is starting to evaporate away and as well as the waters being diverted to a lot of agriculture things and the result is that now the salt lake has the water decreased to a level that is very dangerous to the surrounding environment and right now they are at the level of recommending the citizens in the area to decrease the usage of water. I think what we get from this is that when the government says is just a recommendation a lot of people might not really heed these notices and just go about their day and I think it is important for us to work towards a common good to make sure that our environment stays stable and things like the food chain won't entirely topple because an entire lake is going under, so yeah, I think just making sure you follow your local rules that are in place and just trying the best.

*Albert Zeng:* Cool, yeah, Belinda did you have something to add?

*Belinda Zeng:* Yeah, I was just gonna acknowledge talking about the environment and how to improve the environment is such a needy topic and there are so many different facets to it but I would say give yourself the room to think big. Even google has climate environmental challenges and you can wear different hats as you think about the problem. I think a group of you have thought about new ways to improve renewable energy which I think is super cool like using motion for example as a source and I think just think broadly and think big about ways you can use your ideas, you know, you're young and you might think outside the box and use that, you know maybe in ten ideas nine of them might not make sense but one might be interesting and could have a huge impact. So, I'll just tell you to think big.

*Albert Zeng:* Great, does anyone have anything else to add?

*Valerie Morales:* Yeah, I can add. Thinking about the recent news around celebrities traveling via their planes and having these really large carbon footprints, a lot of people took that information and felt like they were never gonna make that impact so what they do, all of their personal decisions don't matter when it comes to climate change. I find that attitude very pessimistic and I still think that you should think about how you contribute to the world. If you're buying all these new clothes and you think you give them away and people are gonna use them again, it's not true. Most of that clothes are still going to, you know, end up in the landfill, end up being burned and be causing pollution. So really still think about being a conscious consumer, that's important, and use that water bottle. And all of this stuff sounds cheesy but I think it adds up. Particularly when we are buying fewer clothes altogether that's gonna have an impact on how clothes are being produced. If you go to some socially conscious brands and different things like that, I still like to think my individual choices if we are all together will make a big impact. And maybe that is being a little naive but I feel like if we don't have hope and force change nothing is gonna happen and you can keep affecting that way.

# *Afterword*

The 2022 International Cultural Exchange Conference and 2022 Youth International Environment Protection Awareness Conference are products of the combined efforts from students and family. After nearly two months of active preparations, we would like to congratulate everyone on these successful conferences!

Thanks to those who participated in the 2022 Youth International Cultural Exchange Conference, a conference dedicated to improving global youth education and communication among different cultures. We discussed various aspects of national culture and the relationship between them, with presentations about a wide range of topics, such as art, education, personal experiences in high school sports. We would also like to thank those that participated in the 2022 Youth International Environment Protection Awareness Conference, a conference dedicated to provide opportunities for professionals and students to exchange information and ideas about what we can do to help the environment.

We would like to further appreciate our guest speakers and panel speakers for giving us their input and time.

The International Cultural Exchange Conference and Youth International Environment Protection Awareness Conference each had, respectively, over 160 attendees and 120 attendees from the United States, China, Canada, and Australia, and we are grateful for everyone's participation for making this conference possible.